AF541854

The Original Gītā

THE ORIGINAL GĪTĀ

Striving for Oneness

with Comments and Related Verses of the Bhagavad Gītā

GERARD D.C. KUIKEN

MOTILAL BANARSIDASS PUBLISHERS
PRIVATE LIMITED • DELHI

2nd Edition: Delhi, 2015
First Edition: Delhi, 2012

ISBN: 978-81-208-3522-1

MOTILAL BANARSIDASS
41 U.A., Bungalow Road, Jawahar Nagar, Delhi 110 007
8 Mahalaxmi Chamber, 22 Bhulabhai Desai Road, Mumbai 400 026
203 Royapettah High Road, Mylapore, Chennai 600 004
236, 9th Main III Block, Jayanagar, Bengaluru 560 011
8 Camac Street, Kolkata 700 017
Ashok Rajpath, Patna 800 004
Chowk, Varanasi 221 001

Printed in India

by RP Jain at NAB Printing Unit,
A-44, Naraina Industrial Area, Phase I, New Delhi–110028
and published by JP Jain for Motilal Banarsidass
41 U.A. Bungalow Road, Jawahar Nagar, Delhi-110007

Contents

Acknowledgments vii

Preface ix

Part One **Introduction** 1

1 Thought 3
2 Time 12
3 Life-Death 20

Part Two **The Original Gītā**
Date, Correlations, Translation from the Dutch Language, Comments, and Related Verses of the Bhagavad Gītā 29

The Date of the Gītā 31
Correlations 33
1 Philosophical System 36
2 Striving for Oneness 44
3 Striving for Oneness by action 53
4 Striving for Oneness by knowledge 66
5 Striving for Oneness by renunciation of action 76
6 Striving for Oneness by self-restraint 83
7 Striving for Oneness by distinguished knowledge 92
8 Striving for Oneness to the imperishable THAT 98
9 Striving for Oneness by science and wisdom 103
10 The Power of power development 109
11 Striving for Oneness by contemplation of form 111
12 Striving for Oneness by contraction 113
13 Striving for Oneness by the distinction between the observed and the observer 115
14 Striving for Oneness by the distinction of the Three Basic Attributes 121

15 Striving for Oneness to the highest Primordial Spirit 127
16 Striving for Oneness by the distinction in form and formlessness 131
17 Striving for Oneness by the distinction of the Threefold 133
18 Striving for Oneness by liberation through renunciation 137

Glossary 143

Bibliography 157

Index 161

Acknowledgements

For their contributions in various ways to the book, I would like to thank Swami Amaranarda, Professor Bob Bird, Karen Drake, Sondra Grace, Greg Hillis, Professor P. Krishna, Judice Ledeboer, Frans Perquin, Swami Priyavratanand, Professor Ravi Ravindra, Pradeep Sharma, Madhukar Sheth, Rudy Shur, Sigrid Tiefenbrunner, Professor David Gordon White, Fred Wilson, Jaap van der Zanden, and my editor Margaret Dodd. I would also like to thank all the people, friends and opponents, who taught me in my life.

I wish to acknowledge my indebtedness and gratitude to Vimala Thakar for her courtesy in granting permission to quote any explanations I deem necessary from her book *Insights into the Bhagavad Gita*, published by Motilal Banarsidass Publishers, New Delhi, 2005.

Gerard Kuiken

Preface

Why should we study this book? Perennial wisdom is to be found everywhere, in books and seminars dedicated to expanding our understanding of our essential selves and our connection with 'the unlimited Oneness'.

We live in a world that functions by seeming 'dualism', a perspective that keeps us in bondage. In this book, dualism is addressed and shown to be illusionary, since every pair of opposites implies a third element: the notion of a difference implied by both opposites. The discussion of what is an ever-present 'difference' in such a triunity and how it impacts everything we perceive is pivotal to awakening to a new dimension of observation. It is in the unseen difference that we become aware of opposites, such as *long–short, day–night, true–false*.

So what is distinctive about this book? It is essential to realize that each concept has a triune quality as exemplified by the three elements involved: both the opposites and their difference. Is it practical to know this? Yes. Because, by realizing this general law, we can free ourselves from holding to the bias of one particular side. Even though we might not accept the law, we are nevertheless all subject to it, just as we are subject to gravity. And what about that Vastness, that Oneness that often comes up in spiritual works? As what exists is finite, it can be placed in that Vastness by 'distinction', which can only be indicated by a 'limitation'. The process of applying a limitation is inherent in all existence. We ourselves constantly apply limitations unconsciously, and block ourselves from seeing further. A limitation gives rise to a difference, but it will turn out that the limitation has to be repeated again and again since it has no existence by itself.

Dwelling on deepening the understanding of these basic fundamentals, an understanding of space-time might arise. Is this aspect widely discussed in other books? The author does not think so. At this point our work becomes more difficult, but if we can observe these fundamentals in practice for ourselves, we can apply this understanding in our daily lives. We might even study physics and logic to see if it applies there too, since these fields nowadays are in the forefront of the examination of existence. The author has done so, but wanted to go beyond, to understand life in its vastness and not in its limitation. The Vastness is revealed when the limitation is released. But no one else can give us that understanding—an author can only provide road signs, due to the nature of 'the unlimited Vastness'. We might go on reading books and listening to wise people, but we have to investigate for ourselves. Only personal inquiry can bring us understanding and take us beyond limitation.

There are two parts to the book. Part One discusses the essentials of Eastern wisdom in a concise form. It examines the questions: What is thought? What is space-time? What is life-death? The text is kept short so that we can ponder on a few sentences and evaluate for ourselves what has been written. The author's intention was that by distilling the essentials, we would be able to apply them in our daily life and in doing so, that the Vastness and the personal could unite as one. Here a basic understanding of the philosophy of the Gītā can be obtained, providing a foundation for the author's comments on the Original Gītā in Part Two.

Part Two contains the author's translation of the Original Gītā from the Dutch language. It is available in English for the first time. I received the manuscript in 1970 from my teacher Saswitha. That it antedates the Bhagavad Gītā is discussed in the beginning of Part Two. The Original Gītā has 209 verses that can be correlated to 319 of the 700 verses of the Bhagavad Gītā included in the Mahābhārata. As such, it is less than one-third the length of the well-known Bhagavad Gītā, and focuses on the essence of the wisdom of the Gītā. It is called 'original' as it predates other versions of the Gītā into which interpolations, such as the grief of Arjuna as well as some rituals and meditation techniques, were later incorporated. Most importantly, the Original Gītā contains no verses that might validate the caste system, which has been such a detriment to Indian society. In reading and meditating on the text of the Original Gītā we can appreciate the core of its wisdom, recognizing that the Gītā is the science of Life and living.

Short comments on the 209 verses in the Original Gītā can be found. A new translation from the Sanskrit language is given of the 319 verses in the Bhagavad Gītā that correspond to these 209 verses. The Bhagavad Gītā can be found as part of the sixth book of the Indian epic Mahābhārata, and is one of the world's most valuable religious texts. In the Bhagavad Gītā, dialogue takes place between the archer Arjuna [the self], the hero of the epic, holding five arrows [the five senses]; and Kṛṣṇa [the Self], his friend and charioteer, driving the four horses of the chariot [the four elements, the world], when confronted with Life, exemplified as the great battle. These 319 verses are not commented on.

Sanskrit is a classical language and, like every other language, it has its peculiarities. As Sanskrit is also an ambiguous language or, as my friend Ravi Ravindra remarked to me, a flexible language, many different scholarly translations into English exist. While none of these can be considered incorrect, these interpreters usually do not agree with each other on the meaning of the text. I consider myself privileged to have the Original Gītā in my native Dutch, which enables me to select from the various English meanings of a Sanskrit word one that reflects the meaning and philosophical teaching found in the Original Gītā.

Some Sanskrit words, like māyā, are misused or confined to a single meaning in Western popular culture. To show the many meanings and the variability of the language, I have provided a Glossary of 37 germane terms that readers might find useful.

This book has been a labor of love. More than anything, I hope that Part One: Introduction, and my short comments on the Original Gītā in Part Two will be helpful in clarifying the reader's own understanding of the Gītā, and that it will serve as a compass for a voyage of discovery, the goal of which is no less than an understanding of ourselves.

Part One

Introduction

The basics of the philosophical system found in the Gītā are presented showing that man has the potential to realize that he is unlimited and omnipresent. Since we humans seek to understand our world, we start with questions about thought and observation. It is stated that without a limitation there is no existence, and that we become aware of our existence by the observation of differences. Time and space are both coupled and discrete, as discussed in Chapter Two. We experience time in cause and effect, while seeking balance in our lives and pursuing happiness. We do not have to look far, since happiness and understanding are Here and Now within ourselves beyond our self-imposed limitations. Life and death are not separate and should be viewed together; this is examined in Chapter Three, with a short description of the state of inversion, of being dead.

1 Thought

Summary. Existence results from the arbitrary choices of limitations. We discuss the fact that a limitation is imaginary though reflecting one's own cumulative experiences. In the process of observation, it appears that thought is the assimilation of differences manifested by a limitation. The timeless triunity involved has no preference within itself.

We want to understand life. This understanding will be the human conception of life, since man cannot know what lies beyond his own experience. We cannot discern how plants, animals and minerals experience life differently from a human interpretation of their actions. However, we can assume that their life follows the same laws as those throughout the universe. Let us therefore investigate our own existence. It would be useful if a tool were available for this. The tool, the law, would have to be generally applicable if it is to be of value in our search for light on the questions: What is life? Why do we live? Is there a purpose in life? These questions impel us to search for the fundamental process behind our thinking. The observation of our environment, and the objects and beings outside ourselves, occurs through our five senses of sight, smell, hearing, touch and taste, which are all based on distinction—the observation of differences.

In order to observe, we need a limitation. Without one, it is not possible to discriminate. To illustrate this, we can draw a circle. We can then distinguish an inside and an outside. Let a centre point inside the circle represent ourselves as an observer, with the circumference as the observed. The size of the radius is arbitrary and represents the possibilities, experiences, and/or intentions of the observer.

Now it seems that there exist an observer and an observed defined and limited by the circumference. If the radius of the circle shrinks to zero, the point ceases to be an observer, since there is nothing to observe. If the point is removed, there is nothing for the circumference to relate to. From each vantage point, each implies it is the observer and the other the observed, so which is the observer and which is the observed? The impression of an 'I' and a 'you' is because 'I' and 'you' differ. It is due to that difference that the concepts of an observer and an observed arise. Summarizing: the observer and the observed are mutually produced due to their perceived difference. Three related concepts are involved: an observer, an observed, and their difference. This equal and mutual manifestation of each other can be called a triune process. By itself, an observer or an observed is meaningless; in themselves they are nonexistent. Yet both nonexistent unknowns manifest by their apparent difference. A triunity can be constructed as a succession: *observed–difference–observer*. None can be known separately; all are of equal value and form a whole. No exceptions!

A difference is the manifestation of the observed and the observer together. Both do not exist as beings-in-themselves, but are implicitly manifested in the difference caused by a limitation. Through the limitation, the observer becomes aware of himself, due to the assimilation of the difference with the mutually observed. In creating the limitation, the observer is not aware of what is beyond his own limitation. By using induction, we can express the principle: *A limitation gives form to existence as the difference in a triunity. It does not create; it merely makes apparent what already is.*

The observer experiences the limitation as reality and is trapped by it. This reality is then experienced as the living and material world, and beyond that is a non-experienced darkness that is outside the observer's range. Is this range really inaccessible or is it also available to us?

To address that question, we need to see how time enters the picture. In a triunity, all three elements are equally involved, none can be left out, and none is before or after the other. Although mentioned sequentially, no time order is involved in any member of the triunity, which itself is beyond time.

The foregoing discussion stresses the fact that it is an illusion to think that the world operates by dualism, as if each opposite exists-in-itself on its own merit. There is nothing like an observer or an observed existent-in-itself. Nor is there such a possibility that *light* exists without *darkness*, or that there is *short* without *long*. Is the inference then that there is a named triunity, such as *observer–difference–observed, light–difference–dark, long–difference–short*? No, it is only in succession in time that the three in each triunity can be named; two are always concealed in each named member. That is why we should be free from the *thesis–antithesis* opposites, since each has the quality of threeness, and there is always a triune difference involved.

Before we consider further examples and consequences, it is necessary to know that this knowledge has been around since ancient times. My teacher, the Buddhi[1] Priest Saswitha, presented this line of thought in 1953[2] and introduced me to the relevant sources, such as the Bhagavad Gītā and the Tao Tê Ching.

There are a number of verses in the Bhagavad Gītā expressing the idea that one can be free from the pairs-of-opposites (verse 2.4 in The Original Gītā[3]; verse 2.45 in the Bhagavad Gītā). 'Perpetual

[1] Means thinking, understanding, intelligence. Saswitha is a priest from the esoteric school of thought Svābhāvika.

[2] Saswitha, 1953, 1971.

[3] Bhagawad Gita, Jakarta, 1942.

renunciation, free from the pairs-of-opposites, gives liberation of bondages' (5.2, BG5.3). 'The Seers attain the peace of Nirvāṇa, after their twoness has been destroyed' (5.15, BG5.25). And this is not as easy a task as one might think: 'By the delusion of the pairs-of-opposites, arising from attraction and aversion, all beings fall into delusion at their birth' (7.15, BG7.27).

Verse 2 of the Tao Tê Ching is quite explicit. The lines 4–8 discuss how *being* and *non-being*, *difficult* and *easy*, *long* and *short*, *high* and *low*, *tone* and *voice*, *front* and *back* are mutually produced. They are not compared or contrasted, but together form one another, as is particularly noted by Henricks[4] in his Mawangdui text translation of verse 2. Let us dwell a little on the notion of *long* and *short*.

Given a simple length, exemplified by the line A: ——, it is a meaningless question to ask if the line is *short* or *long*. If compared with the size of a human, it is considered as *short*; whereas, if compared with the size of a grain of sand, it is considered as *long*. Neither *long* or *short* can be assigned to the line, just as the line B: ———— is neither *short* or *long*. Only by comparing A with B is A considered as *short* and B as *long*. By being conscious of the difference between A and B, *long* and *short* emerge. All three concepts, *long–difference–short*, come into existence by means of their indestructible unity. None can be eliminated; none comes before or after the other. The triunity is timeless, and therefore it is constant, as the Tao Tê Ching noted in the Mawangdui text (not included in the other Tao Tê Ching texts).

Long and *short* are both recognized by an observer as qualities by becoming conscious of their difference. Only by the difference are the qualities acknowledged without revealing a quality as a 'thing-in-itself'. An independent 'thing-in-itself', an 'absolute', is

[4] Henricks, Robert G., (1992) 1993.

impossible. At first glance, the *thesis–antithesis* pair is noticed, and the difference is unnoticed. We are generally unaware of the timelessness of the unity of three, *long–difference–short*. In a triunity, one element is known and two are unknown: naming them in succession does not reveal the two unknowns. In our existence we cannot do without time, and breaking up the timeless triunity into time consciousness gives us the wrong idea that all three elements can be known. We can work only with the difference; in our example it yields the consciousness of *short* or *long*.

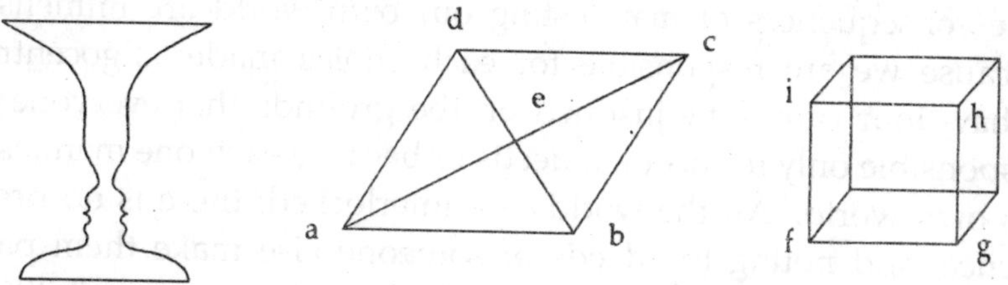

Figure 1.1 Two faces or a goblet; tetrahedrons, pyramids; cubes.

Since by constantly observing, we manifest our existence, let us discuss the triunity further. The manifestation of the difference in the triunity *observer–difference–observed* is according to a chosen limitation. Everyone is aware only of her or his own differences, arising from the particular limitation applied. In the manifestation of the mutual appearance of observer and observed, each one of us constitutes his or her own world. Optical illusions giving quite separate interpretations are well-known[5], such as visually alternating between two faces and a goblet (see Figure 1.1). An engineering illustration is given by the drawings of the rhomboid *abcd* with diagonals *ac* and *bd*, and the cube. It takes but a

[5] Seckel, Al, 2004.

slight effort to perceive the rhomboid with diagonals as various tetrahedrons with bases *abc*, *bcd*, *adc*, and *abd* respectively, or as two pyramids with a vertex *e*; or the second set of lines as a cube with *fghi* in the front or the rear of the cube.

These examples illustrate the fact that the 'difference', in this case the impression gained of the figure, is not dependent only on the 'observed' (the collection of lines) but also on the 'observer', due to an arbitrariness in the choice of limitation. The difference experienced expresses the mutual manifestation of the interaction of the observer and the observed, each in itself nonexistent.

The consequences of manifesting our own world are immense, because we are responsible for each choice made. Egocentric behav- iour cannot be justified on the grounds that everyone is responsible only for his own deeds or because each one manifests his own world. All the worlds are interlocked; there is no preference, and noting the deeds of someone else make them part of our own world, yielding all the accompanying responsibilities we can handle or choose to take on. If we want to be small and blind, it's our own choice, but we can also choose to be compassionate and grow. It's our choice to develop our potential and either embrace or reject our legacy to be fully human.

Our experience of the world outside is filtered through our perceptions; however, our experience can be quite fragmented due to our incomplete awareness of all the differences inherent in our self-imposed limitations. It is also coloured by our personality. That is why communication is so difficult. Everyone is manifesting her or his own world, which differs from anyone else's. Communication is possible only if some common ground is found, and it is not only language that counts. For example, a horse perceived by a horseman, a farmer, a teenager or an Eskimo are all different horses, while the horse itself has no say in the matter, being just a horse.

Unconsciously, we observe ourselves in the observed as assimilators of the difference concerned. We rarely stop doing it. If we do stop, the limitation disappears and we experience the unlimited space that we are. Then there is no distinction between ourselves and others—we are aware that we are One, beyond space and time. The need for experience and growth forces us to constantly and impulsively express ourselves; but the fragmentation due to our self-imposed limitations hinders us from being our true Self, and being aware of our omnipresent unlimited legacy. From the discussion of the triune difference, we have seen that there is non-time; no past, present or future is involved in the triunity. THAT simply IS, without preference, opening us to Life as Oneness.

We look in the world outside the self for freedom and happiness. This is a fruitless attempt, since self-imposed limitations become fixed and so we are trapped. Happiness and freedom are right Here and Now within us if we could allow ourselves to release our limitations. It has been said many times, e.g., by Lester Levenson[6]: 'We are unlimited beings limited only by the concepts of limitation we hold in our minds'. Fred Wilson[7] discusses outer and inner freedom (in his second chapter). Outward freedom implies personal responsibility, and he stresses that freedom should not be confused with license; and on page 129, 'Human beings, in reality, need not be limited in any way—either physically or psychologically—except when we want to express ourselves'.

In expressing ourselves, it could be helpful if we are already conscious of the fact that in the difference, personal desires can be made clear; whence the desires can then be released. That is, not drop them, but understand the motivation behind the desire,

---

6 Levenson, 1993.
7 Wilson, Fred D., 1986.

so we are no longer haunted by desire. Verse 11[8] of the Tao Tê Ching expresses the notion that we usually are unaware of our desire. It is not the being, but the non-being from which desires and their usefulness for man come. The material used to make a cup doesn't matter because it is not the form of the container but its capacity to limit infinite space, its formlessness, that counts, so it can hold your coffee. A small part of clay missing from the lip is of no importance for holding the coffee, but it is if a small part is missing from the bottom. Therefore, if we desire something (the being), let us examine the nothing (the non-being, the emptiness) of our desire, and unite both in the difference for understanding and letting go.

We have to release our self-induced limitations to become whole, to be One, to unite with each other and everything. We are then conscious of what we are—non-finite and united. Still, other limitations are created by myriads of living beings and matter. If we release our limitations and are unlimited and omnipresent, we experience the happiness of that. However, we will also experience the limitations and sorrow of matter and living beings. Therefore, don't interfere with the flow of Life with your personal ego; try to actively follow the flow. In uniting, we can assimilate the difference in *observed–difference–observer* and live a full life in happiness. It's both your own and our common inheritance. We are One with everyone and everything, while we are not harming anything and anyone. The sun still shines irrespective of our thought, yet we are One with the sun and we have cosmic responsibility. We are unlimited, omnipresent with anyone and anything in essence, although our experience is limited and temporal, with the responsibility that comes with the choice of our own measure within ourselves. Let us use the observed to evolve

---

8 'Burn clay and make utensils. Precisely its nothingness gives clay utensils their usefulness! Therefore, its form is favourable but its formlessness is considered as useful'.

ourselves in the assimilation of the difference, thus releasing our self-set limitations.

The mind sets up limitations and controls the consciousness of differences. It even forces us to think. If we try to stop thinking, we feel its power. We may even find it difficult to concentrate on a single item and nothing else, like watching a small balloon disappearing in the blue sky. Our bodies are continually asking for attention, engaging the mind to be constantly alert. The science of brain research is busy examining the tool, but won't find the 'user' of the tool. In the same way, examination of the hammer used as the tool that drives the nail into the wood does not reveal the carpenter or his motivation to this action.

To summarize: Man becomes aware of himself by limitation and experiences that as the awakening of his own world. Does one create his own world? No, because man IS. Yes, because he manifests his own measure.

2 Time

Summary. Time is part of the form world; the formless world is timeless. Both are integral triune parts in their difference, the inversion point holding both in the unfolding of the Now. Existence is the ongoing adaptation in material form to the eternal motion. Time is created in repeated limitations imposed by the mind. The fundamentals of space-time are discussed. Space-time is discrete.

To become conscious of a difference, we have to place a limitation. By this action, we manifest an imaginary stagnation in the flow of eternity. The limitation gives rise to the existent, but doesn't exist itself. It is imaginary; it has to be continually repeated. An example of this is trying to hold a line that divides a piece of paper equally into a left and a right half, by taking a pair of scissors and cutting the paper along the line; the result is, there is no more line, no right and no left. In putting the limitation, the consciousness of the difference is produced and at the same moment space occurs. However, the limitation cannot be maintained; it has to be repeatedly chosen. In these repeated choices, a flow of differences becomes noticeable. This flow we experience as time.

Limitation manifests space, yielding the existent; and, since the manifested limitation cannot be existent-in-itself, it is manifested again and again in each re-choice, yielding time. As a result, we cannot speak about time or space but only of an inseparable 'space-time' consciousness. Space and time exist only together as space-time. As a consequence of the re-choice of limitation, space-time is discrete and as such, finite. Moreover, neither a first cause or a beginning can be given. The broad experiences of daily life, where myriads of limitations manifest the world, hide this fundamental process, and space-time is separated into a continuous space and an endlessly flowing time.

In trying to express ourselves in the ever-changing world we attempt to follow the present, the Now, but we are always late. What we conceive is already past and cannot be altered. That is why the old writings warn us not to distort the course of past causes with personal colours, such as intentions, fears and desires. It only blurs the effects. An illustration might clarify the demand for non-interference. A circle is an ideogram for eternity. A point on this circle marks the present Now. Locally we can draw a straight horizontal line to represent eternity. We are represented in the present Now as a lens to project the differences observed by the limitations manifested in the past (see Figure 2.1).

The manyness observed, the cause, is focused by the observer and projected into the future as the not-yet-observed effect. Figure 2.1 illustrates also that now time is involved in naming the triunity *observer–difference–observed*, which is otherwise timeless. To emphasize: each member is itself a triunity, one named and two unknown and unnamed. One might have thought that the difference could be known as fixed, but it can be conceived that man, the 'observer', is in eternal motion on the line representing eternity. Thus, the 'difference observed' is not fixed, is ever-changing, is in motion. Also remember that the 'observed' is only manifested by setting a limitation, which has no existence in itself. One sets a limitation and becomes aware of existence, but it is already changed; to be aware of the present, a new limitation is needed, forced by the ego to keep pace with the just-manifested observer.

The ego wants us to remain limited, and any change or letting go becomes difficult. Fear may creep in, but in order to be aware of our true selves, we have to accept and release those limitations. Do not blur the conscious difference with feelings of fear. Let us examine these feelings carefully, perceive the difference without personal fear, and be active to equalize it. This enlarges the

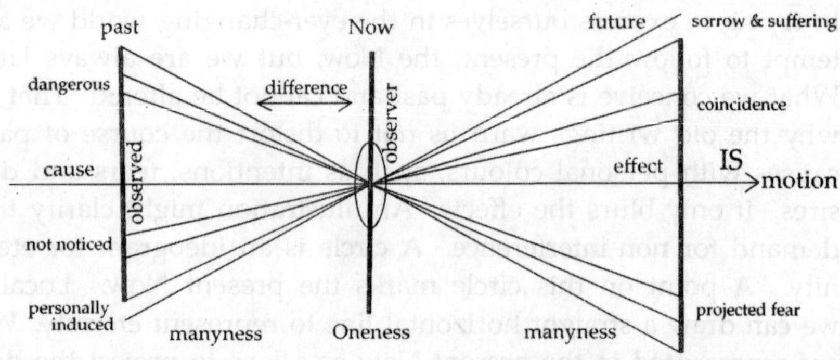

Figure 2.1 The three worlds, cause and effect.

experiences of our mind. The new difference moves the mind and an action is needed to equalize the difference again. There is ever the assimilation and manifestation of differences, flowing from cause and effect.

Human beings are strongly driven by the force of their desires. To list some: humans are driven by animal lust, like maintaining the body and seeking sexual fullfilment; by social lust, like honour, power over and control of others; or by intellectual lust, a desire noticed in many artists and scientists. These are common desires. More unusual are the desires to be helpful to the less fortunate while unnoticed by others, or to be one with the universe. Being such a basic driving force, why is it that most religious writings admonish against yielding to desire? It is because the state of mind is fragmented, ego-centred, denying the wholeness of life. By not being aware of the wholeness of life, many differences are overlooked or added, while nothing can change what is already past, and it is the past that we observe. In living the wholeness, all possibilities are known and there is no need for desire; it has already been fulfilled; simply go with the flow for its manifestation. Being free of our self-set limitations, the materialization of a possibility still involves time from the human perspective, and usually much perseverance is involved.

Desire is also an opportunity to learn what we have missed in the possibilities of the wholeness of life. Look at both sides of the difference that forms the desire to become aware of its underlying nature, just as in the previous discussion on the value of a cup to drink our coffee, its value was found in its emptiness, its capacity to hold the liquid. So to use the opportunity to learn, we can be aware of what it is in our desire we are really asking for, before we act on it. Therefore, consider the antithesis either in the form or formless state and equalize the difference involved.

The lines 11–15 in verse 2[9] of the Tao Tê Ching state that nothing departs from the wise, because he doesn't dwell on the 10,000 things (*wànwù*, the world), including mental concepts like success. He is successful because he is non-doing, which is not at all the same as not acting or *laisser faire*. In fact non-doing is full of action. All actions should be done according to the laws of nature. Full alertness is then required to take into account all the differences manifested, and to respond to them effortlessly in accordance with the flow of cause and effect involved in those differences. We have to take care not to interfere with this process. That is why the Tao Tê Ching in verse 2 tells us that 'the wise man accomplishes and, like heaven, he does not claim the results; therefore the results will not depart from him'.

Figure 2.1 clarifies that induced personal desires, which are not part of the manifested difference, can only result in sorrow and suffering because they do not materialize. Non-observed differences result in coincidences; while differences observed and considered as dangerous for the ego result in fear, which nevertheless might be helpful in facing reality. Non-doing—that is, acting in accordance with all the differences found in a limitation—might

---

[9] The sage resides with non-doing. He is engaged in wordless teaching. He acts and does not keep the actions in mind, just as he does not dwell on the 10,000 things. He accomplishes and, like heaven, he does not claim the results.

be difficult, but is still the wisest action to strive for. Thinking can become the assimilator of differences, uniting past and future in the moving Now. The creations of past and future are imaginary fixations subject to change, and hence cannot be maintained the same as they were in the past.

Man tries to be conscious of the moving Now, and re-establishes a limitation. The re-choices give rise to a repetition of differences, and this discrete re-choice process gives man the awareness of differences in time. Existence is the ongoing adaptation in material form to the eternal motion. In stressful situations we try to keep up with the present, and this results in an awareness that a minute can seem like an hour. On the other hand, if we are at peace with the Now and we are only non-doing, actively being the assimilator of differences, we are in a situation of flow and an hour can seem like a minute; then we do not constantly measure differences in qualities. The measures are merged into our actions and we live the differences. We get an impression of what it is to be ourselves, to be full of happiness. Let us just be, accepting life and living our life as it comes. Complete letting go, completely releasing and being in the Now is impossible due to the demands of the ego and the body, but we can strive for it. Our ego wants to manifest its own world and we are trapped by it. Let it go. Live the cause and effect and do not distort it by our incompletely understood desires, and we will never have to go without anything. Live the Oneness of nature and be it, since All and Nothing is Here and Now.

In the ongoing motion of manifesting differences, the world is manifested as thought by man, according to his personal level of experience. The differences exist only in our thinking and are already gone at the moment of thinking. It is *māyā*, an illusion, the reflection of what is. This holds for everyone and everything, giving the world its reality, but it is still a dream, although lived and thought of as reality, like the hammer that hits your thumb. Please, wake up and be yourself.

There are two areas of illusion, two *māyās* as one. One is manifested by the self and one by the myriads of other selves, but both are still one. The ego that manifested this world can also become enlightened to explore the inheritance of all the forces concealed *within* us, as we accept the unity THAT IS. The law of cause and effect is generally accepted, but it is difficult to realize that the effect is already completely known in the cause. By the assimilation of cause and effect, in equalizing them we can become aware of ourselves in the ever-ongoing revelation, IS.

In equalizing cause and effect, we have to clear our lens. In every new limitation we can examine the result. It does not matter where we start the cleaning process—above, in the middle, left or right—but until there is not a spot left on our lens, it is not clean. We don't have to worry; until our lens is clear we will always get the opportunity to work on it. Finally we will be non-doing, but the work is not finished. In growing in awareness of the process of limitation, its release leads to increased responsibility.

The form world is not aware of the inversion of the mirage in the lens and is not influenced by it; why should we then try to personalize the effect? And in every limitation a form is made knowable, but is not created. Besides, be aware that you deal only with the difference in form (space-time) and the formless (beyond space-time), and work with that difference. The appearance of the effect is formed in the inversion, and is observed only in a repeated limitation yielding a series of time points. From one time point (see Figure 2.1), a line has been drawn as a continuation of time points. You, the middle in cause and effect on such a line, go unnoticed with the motion. The middle can never be annihilated; the line segment of time can be shortened or lengthened, but the middle will always be part of the line segment and you, as the middle, determine the opposing forces.

Figure 2.1 shows the time consciousness of space-time existence; space consciousness is not shown. It is important to keep this in mind because the middle not only shows cause and effect, but also form existence and formless nonexistence. The middle is the inversion point, unseen, always there, changeless, but manifesting the form and formless world both together; it simply IS. It has been named Causeless Cause, THAT, Tao,God, and many other names.

What is the value of this inversion point? Its quality turns out to be: *It is ever there, changeless.* Does that create form and the formless? No, since nothing is created, only manifested. There is no creation; the middle, the Self, always IS. Nothing more, nothing less. *Left–middle–right, form–Self–formless.* No one without the other; no first, no last. A triunity is beyond time, timeless. And there is no superiority or preference: Self, middle, are not confined in space. They are everywhere and nowhere. They are simply IS, beyond space-time. And there is no limitation. IS is the timeless omnipresence. Space-time is created in All Now with the limitation by the mind to manifest the Changeful Changeless.

Starting from an arbitrary point, the notions of left and right are experienced only by drawing a line, but left and right were already part of the starting point, which holds *left–middle–right* unnoticed. The point was chosen from the myriads of other possibilities, so no preference can be found in putting the point somewhere. We seem to be free to manifest space-time anywhere we have in mind. We have fixed ourselves in the expression of form and have forgotten the formless world, in which we also undeniable are. The human and the grain of sand are All IS Nothing manifestations and there is no preference. The grain of sand is also unlimited, omnipresent, and embodies the law. There is no coming, no going, only conversions of the same. In manifestations in time and form there are differences noticed, which by being valued confine man to the form world. Unconsciously, man knows of the formless world but does not know how to connect with it.

3 Life-Death

Summary. In Life, Spirit is beyond space-time and Substance is in space-time. Both are manifestations of IS. Life is called the seen world. Death, the unseen world, can be understood, since what holds for the seen world holds for the unseen world. The Upaniṣads tell us that understanding can be obtained by mind and wisdom alone. In the unseen world, Substance is beyond space-time and Spirit is in space-time. The seen and unseen worlds are Here and Now, described by the ideogram OM.

Let us recall the previous two chapters and reflect on the manifestation of a point. The choice of where to manifest a point is completely free. Having made a choice, we can go anywhere from that point. The point has the characteristics of *left–middle–right, front–middle–back, up–middle–down*. By drawing a horizontal line through the point, a left and a right become obvious. The difference in the dual concepts *left* and *right* is defined by the middle, which is unseen, ever-present, never fixed. It cannot be annihilated in the line segment. Left and right can be interchanged, extended or shortened, but the middle defines both and is an inherent part of the line. Contemplate this example: since there is no preference anywhere, substitute for the middle: Self, and for left–right: Spirit–Substance, and reflect on the Kaṭha Upaniṣad[10] (4.12): 'The Man, of the size of a thumb, resides in the midst, within the Self, of the past and the future the lord; from Him a man hath no desire to hide. This is in truth THAT'. The Self is made conscious due to the mirroring effect of Substance and Spirit, but it cannot be grasped. It is unlimited and untouchable, manifesting itself in expressing Spirit and Substance. It remains simple itself, undisturbed by the limited manifestation of Spirit and Substance. The triunity *Spirit–Self–Substance* is beyond space-time. It IS. It was already, it is not created, and it will

[10] Mead, G. R. S., and Roy Choudhuri, 1896; Olivelle, Patrick, 1998.

not disappear. THAT IS is omnipresent; there is no preference for anyone or anything.

The fact that there is no preference anywhere is expressed in the peace chant of the Īśa Upaniṣad[11]: 'Om! Whole is THAT, whole is this; from whole, whole cometh; take whole from whole, whole remains'. What we learn in the seen world holds equally for the unseen world. Since All IS Nothing, there is no superiority: atoms, minerals, plants, animals, humans are all equally valued. The choice of limitation manifests what already IS. We do not create anything new, but we manifest ourselves in expressing ourselves by the choice of limitation. What we manifest IS already in both worlds. And so it is for everything and everyone else. It is arrogant to think that only man manifests his own world. The atom does, and so does the animal; and there is no superiority anywhere. The notion that man IS can also be read in the Kaṭha Upaniṣad (4.13): 'The Man, of the size of a thumb, like flame free of smoke, of past and of future the lord; he is the same today and tomorrow. This is in truth THAT'. Again: THAT. What is THAT? The answer is not yet explicitly given; only that it is THAT, it is Tao, God, Causeless Cause, Brahma, and so on. Knowing THAT is important, because verse 3.15 explains that 'He who perceived THAT is freed from the jaws of death'; and only by thinking and wisdom can understanding be obtained. 'By intelligence alone is THAT to be obtained, no difference at all is here below; from death to death he goes who here below sees seeming difference' (4.11). Let's try. It can be done, because death complains in verse 4.1 that now and then some wise ones escape from him. How? The wise one looks at the Self within, and uses his wisdom and intelligence.

IS expresses itself in Spirit and Substance or in Substance and Spirit. The Self is the assimilator of both and is the inversion

---

11 Mead, G. R. S., and Roy Choudhuri, 1896.

point in which both are held. Life expresses All and Nothing. Emptiness gives the opportunity for All, and in All, nothing can be added. Since we are forced to express ourselves, we can admit that the Self, the 'middle', is All IS; but equally is implied Nothing IS. The last formulation may give us more freedom in our mind to follow the ongoing motion of the Now, and is more favoured by Zen (with a focus on emptiness). But both expressions are still unbalanced. Balance is achieved as All IS Nothing or Nothing IS All, exemplifying the full meaning of Life IS.

Life IS means that all that appears still remains a unity in spite of the appearance of antitheses. Spirit–Substance is only a form appearance of the unity called man. In the turning point, man's form becomes formless and vice versa. Nothing has happened to the Self; All IS Nothing is only mirrored differently in other states.

The difference always varies and can never become fixed. Since the difference appears to be observable in what we call reality, the form world, we are tempted to think that it cannot be observed in the so-called 'unseen' world. It depends only on our own possibilities, as both the seen and unseen are part of life. We usually live only half of life because of the obtrusiveness of the seen world, but both are Here and Now.

The triunity *seen–Self–unseen* holds as well below (for the seen world) as well as above (for the unseen world). (One in the unseen world is tempted to say 'above as well as below'.) The Kaṭha Upaniṣad verse 4.10 expresses it as: 'What is here (visible), the same is there (invisible); and what is there, the same is here. He who sees any difference here, goes from death to death'. Do not think that 'above' and 'there' are not Here and Now. The world 'above' is unperceived due to the different 'wavelengths' involved.

What we have in mind we try to manifest as Substance. The turning point changes the invisible (Spirit, mind) into the visible (Substance, matter). By assimilation of the difference, the turning point, we strive for equilibrium. If the act is successful every difference disappears, but the mind has gained experience that triggers other actions. Differences are always resolved and manifested at the same time; there is no stopping. Life is an unending motion of the assimilation of differences and yet man simply IS. All IS Nothing has no purpose, no goal; man IS, manifesting the All IS in infinite change, without revealing or changing All. It is an illusion, a dream, and we live it together as the manifestation of All IS—we, plants, minerals, atoms, and so on. And in All IS we are all One together, separated only by the limitations set up by us. In the limitation we look outside, while within us, both the seen and unseen are Here and Now. Since All IS Nothing, we are looking for what we already have and are! Life IS; it is the Now-realization that brings us happiness.

In his expressions of life, by the consciousness of differences man becomes ever more capable of controlling his All IS. It is as if man enlarges his 'All BE' in himself. The triunity of the Self is mirrored in Spirit and Substance to live the unity of All IS. The consciousness of the Self is of equal value to the reflected Spirit and Substance. Nowhere is there a preference in time; triunities are beyond time. No preference is given for man: beyond time holds equally for the molecule. We manifest our own world completely from the possibilities of our limitations. Man is infinite, everlasting, omnipresent, but so are all beings. Man made his own world, his living and his death. If man becomes conscious of All IS Nothing and sees himself in All IS, then death is only an inversion in the mirroring of Substance and Spirit. It is a change of state. The focus on holding to Substance loses its grip and one is inverted without changing the Self. It is like looking in the mirror and saying: 'Hey! That's me' (I am alive) to your image. When you turn away from the mirror and there is no mirror image, are you then saying: 'Hey! I have disappeared' (I am dead)?

Fear accelerates the process to death. Let it go; simply be. In All IS Nothing we do not disappear when we die, and we do not appear or are created when we are born. We simply are, infinite, Changeful Changeless. In dying we experience a change of state, and of course all is changed; space-time is also inverted. It might be difficult, but a good understanding of 'life' gives us the opportunity to understand 'death'.

In life, man's spirit is unseen, while man experiences Substance, the material world. In death, the Substance is unseen, while the Spirit is experienced. In the inversion, the middle, the turning point, man remains untouched, IS only, and mirrors the inversion like a lens. In this transition, space-time becomes beyond space-time: *past–present–future* are not relevant. We cannot say: 'I will visit my friend tomorrow'. No, the experiences collected in Substance are there the moment they are thought of. The Substance world behaves like the world of the mind in life. The manifestation of our world is exclusively our own. If other influences are not allowed, they do not appear. In life anyone can disturb us, even if we don't want it. In death, no one can disturb us, unless we allow it.

In death, there is no past, present or future; only the ongoing Now. The time-line in Figure 2.1 is seen from eternity and can be represented by a point, so that we cannot mark a past, present or future. A movie projected on a screen has no substance, no depth, no 'body', is intangible, but seems quite real. The beyond-space movie we reflect on the unseen screen can be pictured by a circle on which the collected experiences of a life can be shown (see Figure 3.1).

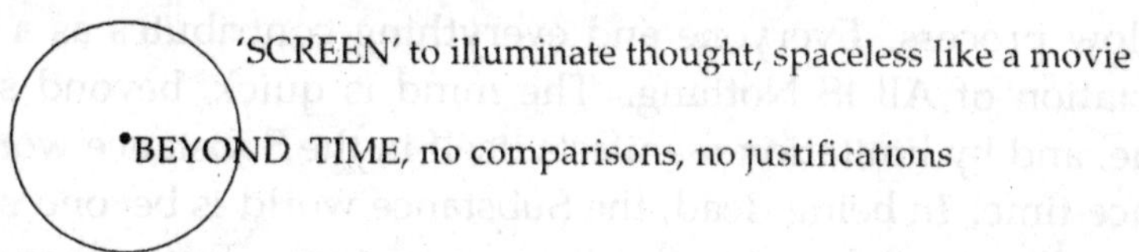

Figure 3.1 Being dead.

The combination of Figures 3.1 and 2.1 gives us O I I I, the picture of the word OM (see Figure 3.2). Clearly, OM explains death and life. This is also found in the Upanisads. In answer to the question: 'What is beyond right and wrong, beyond past and future?' (Kaṭha Upaniṣad 2.14), the answer is: 'The word that all seek. It is OM'. (Kaṭha Upaniṣad 2.15). Its meaning is enlightened further in the Māṇḍūkya Upaniṣad[12]: 'That OM, the word which never dies—this all its meaning is. What was, what is, what will be, all is but OM; what else besides which triple time transcends, that, too, is OM'.

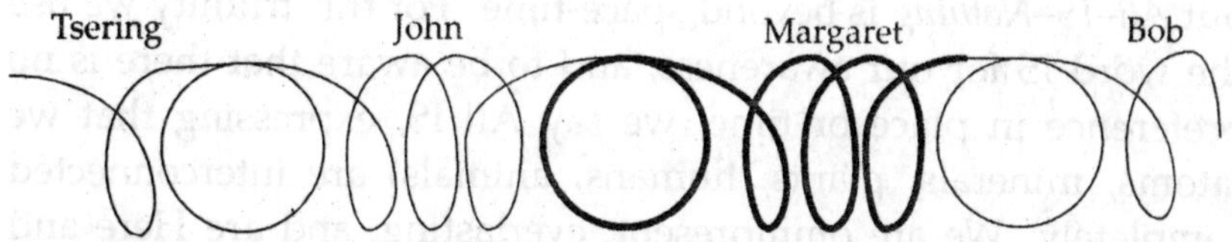

Figure 3.2 OM: Changeful Changeless.

Our mind in life has control over past, present and future. It is not bounded in time, but to manifest a thought the characteristics of the Substance world demand time evolution. The qualities in Substance, the material world, are fixed in respect to the operations of the mind. The evolution in time of the material world is

[12] Mead, G. R. S., and Roy Choudhuri, 1896.

a slow process. Everyone and everything contributes as a manifestation of All IS Nothing. The mind is quick, beyond space-time, and by limitation manifests itself in the Substance world, in space-time. In being dead, the Substance world is beyond space-time, illuminated by the Spirit in space-time. Every thought is immediately illuminated and lost the moment the thought has gone. The Spirit is now in space-time and displays and balances the experiences gathered in life. Wishes, considerations, thoughts that have not been materialized in the space-time world are now illuminated. They cannot be held back, since the illumination is beyond time. Our obsessions will be there and will be released, since there is no past or future to compare with, only acceptance of what is revealed. All IS has become Nothing IS, and the transition from All to Nothing does not affect the ongoing Now, which is felt as duration.

Space-time is discrete, and the limitation manifests only what IS, but it is nonexistent itself. Space-time is discrete in revealing All. In IS, both All and Nothing can be explained by limitation, but *All–IS–Nothing* is beyond space-time. For this triunity we use the word IS for our awareness; and to be aware that there is no preference in place or time, we say All IS, expressing that we (atoms, minerals, plants, humans, animals) are interconnected completely. We are omnipresent, everlasting, and are Here and Now in trillions of variations in All IS. To experience that, we have to release our own limitations, our fears and desires, and live our heritage Here and Now. Figure 3.3 summarizes the flow of life and death and we might deduce the old symbols of life from the figure.

How can we experience the unseen world and what can we expect? 'The wise does not look outside but turns his eyes away to the Self within' (Kaṭha Upaniṣad 4.1). One has to become quiet. This is exercised in the yogi state of 'dead man'. One becomes unaware of one's own body and becomes silent. One's mind-wave

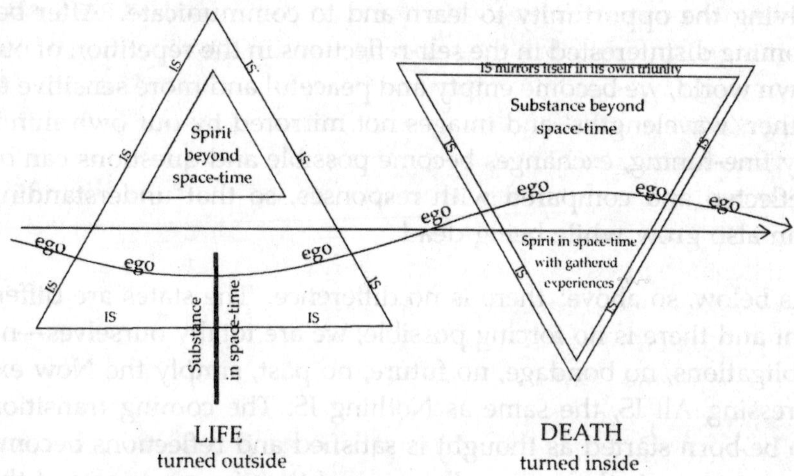

Figure 3.3 Changeful Changeless in IS.

patterns subside and mirror beyond space-time. Since I have not mastered that exercise[13], I can report the dying, death and birth experiences of my teacher, the yogi[14] Saswitha. Below is a précis of these experiences as he discusses them in his book[15], *Dying and Being Dead*, written in Dutch.

The beyond-time (non-time) of mind is converted in time giving the feeling of duration: *past–present–future* has been collapsed into one. What we think is immediately illuminated, as if the Spirit illuminates a particular experience in the hologram of our total experiences. The 'inside' thought is seen as the 'outside' world. We see our own world. We are totally occupied with ourselves and therefore not lonely. If we meditate, nothing is viewed. In this world no shadows can be found. The time consciousness of the Spirit helps us to become conscious of the state of death,

---

13 We will experience the unseen world anyway when dying.

14 A yogi is capable of being in both the seen and unseen worlds, while being in one.

15 Saswitha, 1974.

giving the opportunity to learn and to communicate. After becoming disinterested in the self-reflections in the repetition of our own world, we become empty and peaceful and more sensitive to other 'wavelengths' and images not mirrored by our own mind. By fine-tuning, exchanges become possible and questions can be reflected and compared with responses, so that understanding can also grow while being dead.

As below, so above: there is no difference. The states are different and there is no forcing possible; we are totally ourselves—no obligations, no bondage, no future, no past, simply the Now expressing All IS, the same as Nothing IS. The coming transition to be born started as thought is satisfied and reflections become scarce; there is then some allowance of time in non-time and the mirroring in mind becomes weak. As the transition comes near, as dying does in old age, thought becomes more limited, more fixed, and we turn into ourselves with no special expression, only with seeing inside and the thinking chakra. Our feelings try to find 'vibrations' that we like or need from our next father and mother to express IS in a new life form; so that the Spirit can assimilate differences in space-time in enveloping IS.

Part Two

The Original Gītā

Date, Correlations, Translation from the Dutch Language, Comments, and Related Verses of the Bhagavad Gītā

The Date of the Gītā

There is an enormous literature about the Bhagavad Gītā [BG], also about dating the BG, but there seems to be a rough consensus that the BG was inserted[16] into the Mahābhārata between the third[17] or the second[18] century BCE (Before Common Era) and the first centuries CE[19]. Most scholars date the BG around 150 BCE, but one has to consider that there was an oral tradition, dating the BG further back in history. Khair[20] gives a table with suggested dates varying between 3101 BCE[21] to the third century CE. The date of the Original Gītā [OG] is older than the BG. This might not be hard to accept; however, to define a century BCE is almost impossible and cannot be substantiated by old manuscripts, but can be by considering its content. The OG is not in rhymed verse, and it is remarked[22] that in the original form, the BG was in unrhymed Sanskrit verse. A summary of modern research on the two views that in practice are tenable about the BG can be found in Brockington[23]. To quote Brockington[24], 'either it [the BG] is an integral part of the *Mahābhārata* and directed pragmatically to Arjuna's situation, or it is a later insertion (which includes the possibility of a later expansion of a brief original) developing a philosophically and theologically significant message from its *Mahābhārata* context'. Clearly the OG

---

16 In the Mahābhārata there is evidence that the BG in its present form was not part of the epic. Belvalkar, S. K., Vol. 2, 1969, pp. 136–7, passage quoted in Narla, V. R., 2010, p. 117.

17 Malinar, Angelika, 2007, p. 14.

18 Patton, Laurie L., 2008, p. xxv.

19 White, David G., 2009, p. 38.

20 Khair, G. S., 1997, pp. 16, 17.

21 The mythological year of the war described in the Mahābhārata. Bhandarkar [Bhandarkar R. G., Vol. 1, 1933, p. 365.] is convinced that the Mahābhārata is not a historical work.

22 Johnson, W. J., 1994, p. xxiv.

23 Brockington, J. L., 1998, pp. 267–271.

24 Brockington, ibid., p. 269.

is considered here as the candidate for the brief original. The original unrhymed Gītā had to be modified to become rhymed in verse form with four lines of eight or eleven syllables, the verse metre that is found in the BG. In the OG there is no reference to the war as depicted in the Mahābhārata epic. To incorporate the OG into the Mahābhārata, the despair of Arjuna and the set-up of the battle were added (BG1.1–2.10). There is no author known of the OG, Kṛṣṇa and Arjuna are not there, sacrifice and devotion to anyone is not found in the OG; only a consistent philosophy is presented. The OG lacks the four-caste system and its discrimination.

One might be able to appreciate that the OG is genuine while studying its content. It is also found that the corresponding 319 verses of the BG closely resemble the OG verses. As a consequence of their correspondence with the OG, these 319 verses form the core[25] of the BG. Even in these core verses some reference to devotion and faith is added. The layer of devotion and faith in the BG shows that these interpolations are of a late date[26]. Surendranath Dasgupta[27] dated the BG as pre-Buddhistic. That might be assumed of the OG, but not of the BG[28]. In OG5.15 the word *nirvāṇa* is found and occurs six times[29] in the BG. The occurrence of the term *nirvāṇa* poses no problem, as it is not

25 Minor, Robert N., 1982, p. xxi: 'The "original story", which cannot be clearly known, probably constitutes the central story of the epic as we have it and comprises about one-half of the text. Its origin may go back as far as the eight or ninth century B.C.'

26 The Sāṃkhya and Yoga layers precede the Vedāntic elements but the *bhakti* [devotion] layer definitely comes last. Mislav Ježić, 1986, quoted in Brockington, ibid, p. 269.

27 Dasgupta, Surendranath, Vol. 2, 1952, p. 552.

28 '... the BG is the result of development of the religious and philosophic speculation that prevailed before the rise of Buddhism.' Bhandarkar, R. G., Vol. IV, 1929, p. 39.

29 BG2.72, 5.24–26, 5.15.

only a Buddhistic[30] term but also a pre-Buddhistic Kāla philosophy term[31]. According to Minor[32], the origin of the BG may go back as far as the eight or ninth century BCE, which might be considered as the date for the OG.

Correlations

The Bhagavad Gītā [BG] is a book that formulates the science for obtaining a deep understanding of the wholeness of Life, of the nature of ultimate reality. It is part of the sixth book, known as the Bhishma Parva, of the Indian epic Mahābhārata[33], the largest epic ever written. The Mahābhārata is about three times the size of the Bible or seven times the size of the *Iliad* and the *Odyssey* combined, those two most important works of Homer in ancient Greek literature, and contains about 100,000 verses. The BG has only 700 verses. This is the standard number of verses; the highest number quoted by commentators of the Gītā is 745. The total number of extra stanzas actually found from a number of other BG manuscripts are 19 whole stanzas, 10 half-stanzas, and 4 stanzas copied from another source. These can be found in the critical edition of the BG[34], but they are not considered as authentic[35]. In Zaehner[36] most of the extra stanzas can be found, as well as in Minor[37]. Yet, in spite of its short length, the BG is one of the great religious classics of the world. To align the Original Gītā [OG] with the Mahābhārata, it seems natural that

30 The generally accepted date of Buddha's death about 486 BCE has been recently reconsidered to be 375–355 BCE. Patrick Olivelle, 1998, p. 12.

31 S. K. Belvalkar, Vol. 2, 1969, 156n. Quoted in Minor, Robert N., ibid., p. 99.

32 Minor, Robert N., ibid., p. xxi.

33 Ganguli, Kisari Mohan, 1981, pp. 29–98.

34 The Bhagavadgītā, edited by S. K. Belvalkar, 1945.

35 The Bhagavadgītā, ibid., pp. xxi–xxiii.

36 Zaehner, R. C., 1969.

37 Minor, Robert N., 1982.

interpolations were necessary to have consistency with the battle story of that great epic, with the chapter headings dropped. This tripled the size of the BG compared with the OG, and resulted in the well-known form of a dialogue between Arjuna and Kṛṣṇa. Many scholars[38] are convinced that there are interpolations in the BG. Khair[39] has given summaries of the views of some representative scholars, while Sinha[40] has no doubt on historical grounds that many verses are interpolated. It should therefore be of no surprise that the OG is much shorter than the BG, and is concentrated on the philosophical and practical essentials of Life and living, without any reference to a battle or warriors. There are also no lines implying devotion to Kṛṣṇa, since Kṛṣṇa as a teacher is of a later date. With the interpolation of 381 verses, the devotional part has become overwhelming. To quote White[41]: 'Of course, the Bhagavadgītā was, before all else, the manifesto of an emergent sectarian theism, which argued for the superiority of the path of devotion to a personal god over the inferior paths of action and knowledge'.

The caste system (BG4.13) is not found in the corresponding verse OG4.9, a system that seems to be a deterrent to the unity of the society of India. To quote Minor[42]: 'Central to the Gītā is its concern that the caste structure be maintained. By declaring that the fourfold caste system was created by Kṛṣṇa (BG4.13), it also held that it was better not to teach the truth to people if it caused them to depart from their duties (*varṇa-dharma*), which were determined by their place in the social structure, i.e., their

---

38 Minor, ibid., pp. xxxii–xliii, has given a historical account of scholars on an original Gītā. His conclusion is that the evidence for interpolations is not solid and therefore he considers the Bhagavadgītā as a well-preserved scripture by an unknown author added to the Mahābhārata.

39 Khair, G. S., 1997.

40 Sinha, Phulgenda, 1987.

41 White, David G., 2009, p. 40.

42 Minor, Robert N., 1986, pp. 3, 4.

caste (BG3.26, 29)'. Where in OG18.11 of the Original Gītā one is reminded to "be oneself and others be themselves", BG18.41–48 refer to the duties of caste as one's inherent-self-nature-born duties. During seminars held in 1992 and 1993, Vimala Thakar[43] remarked: 'You would be surprised that, till twenty-five or thirty years ago, women were not supposed to study or recite the Gītā. It was only for the renunciates, *saṃnyasins*. The householders too were not encouraged to study the *Gītā*, because it was feared that their interest in family life would disappear'. Also, in BG18.67–71, Kṛṣṇa gives the advice not to reveal these most secret teachings to those who do not want to listen, do not have the right qualities, or are against him.

In Part Two, the stanzas in the OG are commented on with reference to Part One. The corresponding verses in the BG are given in a new translation. It is found that a literal translation very close to the original stanza is possible with the words provided in the classical dictionaries. The 319 corresponding verses in the BG can be considered as the core of the classic BG. A full account of this new translation is given in Kuiken[44]. Words in square brackets in this translation are needed for the English, but do not occur in the Sanskrit version of the BG. A selection of consulted English translations can be found in the Bibliography.

With each verse of the Original Gītā the related verse or verses in the Mahābhārata Bhagavad Gītā are given in italics. The BG-number at the end of these verses refers to the number of the verse in the Bhagavad Gītā.

43 Thakar, Vimala, 2005, p. 192.
44 Kuiken, Gerard D. C., 2012.

1 Philosophical System

Over whom you should not mourn, you have mourned, yet you speak words of wisdom. For the dead and the non-dead, the wise do not mourn. BG2.11

1.1 Over whom you should not mourn, you mourn. For the dead and for the non-dead, the wise do not mourn.

Comment: The Original Gītā starts directly by expressing that Life IS. Life manifests itself in myriad forms. We adhere to those forms and fear the non-form. The non-form is beyond space-time and limitations can be released more easily being dead than being non-dead, but both are equally important. The first verse points that out too by not referring to the living and non-living, but to the dead and the non-dead. Our egos want to hold to what is known, and although we say the dead have gone to a better world, we doubt it and have fear. Also in missing our dead friends and relatives we mourn in the process of adjusting our ego to the new situation, but this will not change Life. Life will continue to reflect itself in the dead and the non-dead. The verse also expresses that our thinking is usually from our limited time view, forgetting the ongoing eternity of Life while holding onto the temporal.

Yet never have I not been, nor you, nor these rulers of men; and neither hereafter from here beyond, we all shall not be. BG2.12

1.2 Yet never have I not been, nor you; and neither hereafter from here beyond, we all shall not be.

Comment: Life has no beginning or end, although form manifestations of Life have a beginning and an ending. This verse becomes personal and expresses that Life is not limited to the 'I' or the 'you', and it refers to wholeness by changing the 'I' and 'you' to 'all we'. It shows also the eternity of being, that in its temporal form expression has to be equivalent to the eternal form expression. So, since being eternal, it is not wise to mourn over the form change of Life, over the form manifestation of Life is in its ongoing change of the same.

Just as in this body of the embodied [there is] childhood, youth and old age, so [there is] also obtaining another body, the wise one does not become confused by this. BG2.13

1.3 Just as to the ego in this body childhood, youth and old age happen, so it also obtains another body.

Comment: The ego is here considered as a sort of 'I' that reflects the ongoing life in a material body and after death in another body. Childhood, youth and old age are part of the body, but not of the ego that is ongoing reflecting itself in a life, cyclic in time, and in a death, cyclic in not time. In doing so, Life improves its manifestation by repetition, the ongoing conversion in Life of the dead and non-dead. We have to go slowly through the form expressions of Life to learn and to balance *Spirit–Matter* in the ongoing assimilation of the difference, thereby expressing and investigating ourselves.

Material contacts, Arjuna, causing cold and heat, pleasure and pain; coming and going, [are] not lasting. You must endeavour to endure them, Arjuna! BG2.14

1.4 Now the contact with the material world causes cold and heat, pleasure and pain; they come and go; they are temporary.

Comment: The qualities of life in a material body are mentioned. All physical sensations are impermanent, and a source of learning where our imbalances are, in particular the pains we do not like. We have not only to endure them, but to look at them, and often they turn out afterwards to be big gifts of Life for understanding. In the ongoing manifestations of Life in death and non-death, the impermanent experience of pleasure and pain will be ongoing too, until one understands that pleasure and pain are self-induced and changing in the flow of Life. The ego collects those experiences lived, and the realization of 'I-ness' in being alive in the form can be relaxed by realizing that in being dead the same law applies, since life and death are only reflections of the ego.

For the non-being no existence is found, nor is nonexistence found for the being. The nature of these two has also been seen by the perceivers of truth. BG2.16

1.5 For the non-being no existence is found, nor nonexistence is found for the being. The difference between these two has also been seen by those who perceive the truth.

Comment: Logically it seems that two easy equivalent propositions are given: 'no existence in non-being' ('a') and its negative, or 'no nonexistence in being' (non-'a'). It is like the discussion in Part One of *long* and *short* in the general description of Spirit and Substance. Neither one has an existence as a thing-in-itself. The positively and negatively formulated statements emphasize that in the difference, both are included to form the triunity *Spirit–difference–Substance* and that only in the difference both are manifested, yet neither reveals Spirit or Substance. The ego reflects itself in death or in life, but to death no existence can be allotted nor can in life nonexistence be allotted. The difference in both is seen by those who have seen the truth of the eternal ongoing ego.

Indeed, know [that] THAT [is] indestructible, by which all this is diffused! The destruction of that imperishable, no one is able to accomplish. BG2.17

1.6 Know however that THAT is indestructible, whereby all this is pervaded. The destruction of that imperishable, no one is able to accomplish.

Comment: THAT is not personal. THAT is indefinite as the ego is indefinite, but the ego becomes observable in the living being as well as in the dead. THAT causes the difference in living and dead, and has as such no independent existence in itself and is therefore indestructible. Besides, the verse states that All IS, and that there are only conversions in All IS, called THAT. The manifestations of Spirit and Substance in THAT do not reveal IS or THAT. All is pervaded by THAT and even an assumed destroyer or creator is part of All, and therefore it is impossible to create or to destroy the imperishable.

These bodies having an end, are said [to be] of that what is embodied, of the eternal, imperishable, and immeasurable. Therefore fight, Arjuna! BG2.18

1.7 These bodies have a core that is eternal, imperishable, and immeasurable. Therefore fight.

Comment: The realities of Spirit (unobservable) and Substance (observable) are called bodies and only manifest in the difference, the kernel, without revealing Substance and Spirit. In the triunity *Spirit–difference–Substance*, none can be missed, none has preference, nor is one before the other. So the triunity is beyond time and therefore eternal and indestructible. Measuring is the assimilation of differences and involves time. Time is not found in the triunity *Spirit–difference–Substance*, so it is also not measurable. It is worth fighting for the understanding of the kernel, the difference, and not holding onto the delusion of the dualities, the two bodies, Substance and Spirit. If we were temporal, perishable and measurable, the fight would end when knowing the things.

He is not born, nor does he ever die. Nor, having been like this, will he [ever] not be once more. Unborn, eternal, everlasting, and ancient, this is not killed when the body is being slain. BG2.20

1.8 This one is not born, nor does he ever die. Nor, since he has been, will he ever not be. Unborn, everlasting, perpetual, he is not killed when the body dies.

Comment: This, the difference, the kernel, is not born nor does it ever die, because the difference is only manifested as a result of a limitation. It is not created, it is only manifested and it proves that All IS. As the ego mirrors the eternal ongoing life, he is not born nor does he ever dies, and since he has not been, he will never be. The kernel, the difference, remains as a potentiality in All IS. Nothing is therefore created or destroyed; simply Life IS, ongoing in myriads of manifestations and dissolutions, expressing Oneness without revealing IS. It is like a mirror that is there, does not die and takes its presence only due to observation.

As man casting away worn-out garments takes other new ones, so the embodied one, casting away worn-out bodies, encounters other new ones. BG2.22

1.9 As man, after casting away his worn-out garments, takes other new ones, so the ego, after casting away worn-out bodies, goes over into other new ones.

Comment: This verse expresses the continuity of Life where man is one of the many manifestations that will change in form. This is the view seen from human perspective. The Life force found in the ego has to manifest itself in Spirit and Substance in the ongoing assimilation of the difference to balance imbalances and to release the chain of limitations. The ego is changeless but the mirrowing is in ongoing change, as seen from life as well as from death.

This is not to be cut, burned, wetted, and also not to be dried. Lasting, all-pervading, stationary, unmoving and ancient is This. BG2.24

1.10 'THE' is lasting, all-pervading, stationary, perpetual.

Comment: This verse is correcting the particular human view that might have come up that the ego changes cloths. So, a more general and abstract name for the Life force, the continuity of Life's manifestations, is called 'THE', the triunity *life–ego–death* that is stable, all-pervading, immovable, eternal, beyond time.

Then it is not limited to a particular manifestation in the abstract triunity *THIS–THE–THAT*, beyond space-time, and properties and attributes cannot be assigned.

This is called unobservable, unthinkable, immutable. Therefore, knowing this, you should not mourn. BG2.25

1.11 'THE' is called unobservable, incomprehensible, immutable Therefore, do not mourn for anybody.

Comment: Life IS, expressing form and formless or life and death in 'THE'. Why do we adhere to the form side? We mourn when the form is gone from our observation, while the ISness of Life is not changed. A conversion of Life forms is not seen by us as a continuation. If we could loosen our one-sided orientation to the form side of Life and be more in the middle, we could release our fixation to form or not form and become free. Then we are balanced in the freedom of Life's ISness, and we call it happiness.

Death for the born is certain and certain is the birth of the dead. Therefore, when the matter is inevitable you should not mourn. BG2.27

1.12 As death for the born is certain, certain is the birth of the dead. Because of this, you should not mourn for the inevitable.

Comment: To be born means to make observable what was unobservable to us. The force to be born is the driving force to assimilate the difference expressed for not being in the middle, for not being in the ISness of Life. To be born, we have the opportunity to clean up the imbalances noticed in that difference. In doing so, the beyond space-time of death becomes space-time for assimilating the differences. But the born cannot hold on to create space-time indefinitely, and death of the born is certain. To mourn for what is certain is holding onto limited time expression, and we should not do so. Observable and unobservable are only names given from the perspective of the living. Seen from the middle there is no birth or death, only the ISness of Life. In understanding this, fear about birth and death can be released and we can live the vast stillness, the silence, in peace with Life. The verse is often interpreted as stating reincarnation. Reincarnation is a one-sided view of the living, appreciating only the observable temporal as important.

Unobservable are the beginnings of the beings, observable are their mid-states, Arjuna, unobservable are also their endings. Why then a lamentation? BG2.28

1.13 Unobservable is the beginning of the beings, observable their mid-state, unobservable also their ending. Why then mourn?

Comment: Observable is only the Now, not what is before or after. This verse teaches us that the ego is ongoing. It expresses the moving now that shows past and future as a form shift in the now. The 'turning points' of the beginning and ending of beings is without beginning or end. From the time perspective we see birth and death, from the eternity perspective the changeful changeless now. When we become conscious of our real value, then we are always ongoing in the now, without fear for the death or fear for the re-embodiment.

2 Striving for Oneness

This intelligence is to you declared in [the philosophy of] Sāṃkhya. But learn this regarding Yoga! Disciplined by which intelligence, Arjuna, you shall cast off the bond of action. BG2.39

2.1 If you possess this, you shall yourself cast off the bonds of action.

Comment: This, the Sāṃkhya philosophy in the Bhagavad Gītā, discusses Life as a whole. While we are involved in daily life, being one-sided in Substance or in Spirit, we do not yet have the overview and understanding of the whole. We are driven by the force of life, by relationships, by personal interpretations. We do not see life as the whole that we are, and we are not yet capable of using our power of self-realization. We have a long way to go and the Bhagavad Gītā takes us deeper into this theme. When we are able to understand and use this wisdom in our lives, then there is no bond to a personally driven action, since we are ourselves in the wholeness of Life, simply assimilating the differences Life gives.

In this effort there is no loss or decrease found. Even very little of this practice protects from great danger. BG2.40

2.2 Striving for Oneness causes no loss in the effort. It is never in vain. Every attempt is beneficial.

Comment: In our striving for Oneness every effort, our good and wrongdoings, contributes to our understanding. Learning to see the error, learning to accept the inevitable consequences of cause and effect, while trying to understand the deeper meaning, will help us in becoming ourselves. So every effort contributes to correcting our incomplete view and there is no loss, only gain, in our growth. Loss and gain are our notions; they do not apply to the whole.

The ignorant ones, who propound this flowery speech, enamoured the letter of the Veda, Arjuna, thus saying, 'There is nothing else'. BG2.42 To those attached to pleasure and mastery, whose minds [have been] plundered by this, resolute insight in contemplation is not granted. BG2.44

2.3 The letter of the Vedas, saying: 'There is nothing else', produces ignorant ones. The spirit, however, engenders contemplation.

Comment: Everything is always changing as the manifestation of the Changeless. All is relative and changing, so holding onto a fixed point, following the letter and not the spirit, is the standpoint of ignorant ones. Wise ones contemplate each and every standpoint, see beyond, and are open to new insights.

The range of the Vedas concerns the Three Basic Attributes; be without the Three Basic Attributes, Arjuna: free from the pairs-of-opposites; always have stability in reality; free from securing acquisitions! Be possessed of the Self. BG2.45

2.4 The Vedas discuss the Three Basic Attributes; be free from the Three Basic Attributes: the pairs-of-opposites; the instability in reality; acquisition. Seek the possession of the Self.

Comment: As discussed in Part One, only in the difference do we name the opposites. In themselves none exists and as we are easily deluded by the pairs-of-opposites, not seeing the triunity involved of *opposite–difference–opposite*, we are in imbalance in one or the other opposite. In the difference we create and live our own world, always changing; it is called reality: Māyā. We are unstable in reality if we do not accept that all manifestations are ever-changing triune differences yielding space-time without revealing the unmanifest. In daily life we need possessions, and as long as our possessions do not possess us, there is no acquisition and then they are our helpers in daily life.

As much use [as there is] in a reservoir submerged with water on all sides, so much [is the use] in all the Vedas for the brahmin who knows. B2.46

2.5 As guidelines for contemplation, all the Vedas are of great use.

Comment: For understanding reality and Life, all scriptures, sciences, and spiritual writings everywhere in the world are of value and are useful. This verse emphasizes that there are many sources of knowledge and understanding, and that this stanza not only refers to the knowledge found in the Vedas, a part of India's rich spiritual culture.

Your authority [is] in action only, not at any time in the fruits. Let the fruit of action not be your motive. Let there be no attachment to non-action! BG2.47

2.6 Act only. The fruit of action should not be a motive. Forget non-action.

Comment: Following a teaching [a Veda] is incomplete; we have to act, to apply the teaching. To act, we have only to follow cause and effect without personally adding wishes or fears, and evaluate what life in the motion of cause and effect tries to teach us. Forget non-action, since the law of cause and effect will work anyway.

Fixed in Yoga perform actions! Having abandoned attachments, Arjuna, having become constant in success and failure, [that] constancy is called Yoga. BG2.48

2.7 Equanimity is striving for Oneness.

Comment: In assimilation of the differences perceived in the motion of life, in cause and effect, we balance the opposites. We are in equanimity, and in this balance the opposites disappear and we obtain Oneness in the never-ending process of the assimilation of differences.

He who is disciplined in intelligence casts off here both [actions] done well and done badly; therefore, discipline yourself for Yoga! Skill in actions [is] Yoga. BG2.50

2.8 He who strives with his intelligence for Oneness casts off both good and evil here.

Comment: In striving for Oneness by assimilating the differences in cause and effect, there is no labelling of good or evil. The totality of the process is of importance, not only the good side. It is the ongoing motion of life that we have to follow, without stating a purpose, without labelling.

When your intelligence will overcome the confusion of fallacy, then you will obtain indifference to that which is to be heard and what has been heard. BG2.52

2.9 When your intelligence (Buddhi) overcomes the confusion of fallacy, then you are contemplating in truth, without the disturbance of other explanations.

Comment: It is a delusion to think in pairs-of-opposites. We have to understand that thinking involves *opposite–difference–opposite* as a triune entity, while realizing that time is not involved, since none comes before or after in the triunity. Having overcome this idea of opposites and having contemplated in oneself the Oneness of the threeness, we are in truth, also understanding that time manifests from the Now. The Now incorporates *past–present–future,* since there is no independent past, present or future. Realizing the long road to this understanding, overcoming the confusion of fallacy, we will not be disturbed by other explanations.

When a man casts off all desires, Arjuna, [that are] concealed in the mind, satisfied only in and by the Self, then one is called steady in knowledge. BG2.55

2.10 Restrain desire, seek satisfaction in and by the Self, then you are steady in knowledge.

Comment: A warning is given here to apply the knowledge obtained so that there is a firm basis of understanding. Therefore, we have to restrain the desire to go too fast; we have to be satisfied in the Self by the Self. Let us reconsider our old thinking, that thinking in pairs-of-opposites, and strive for Oneness with the help of the Self.

He whose mind is unshaken in sorrows, whose desires for pleasure are gone, who is free from passion, fear and anger, is called a hermit steady in thought. BG2.56

2.11 When passion, fear and anger are conquered, steadiness in thought results.

Comment: Even if we have succeeded in understanding the Sāṃkhya philosophy, we have also to restrain the passion for this knowledge. Apply and test in practice the newly obtained knowledge for its correctness, so that the fear of the steadiness of the new knowledge will disappear and there will be no anger raised in you if confronted with other 'knowledge', since your steadiness in thought is well-founded.

Indeed, Arjuna, even for a wise man who is striving, the harassing senses forcibly carry away the mind. BG2.60

2.12 Harassing senses forcibly carry away the mind.

Comment: Only if we are attached to something, including knowledge and wisdom, can the senses be stimulated in such a way that our thinking is no longer reasonable. So learn to restrain the senses to become free from the imprisonment of attachment.

Restraining them all, he should sit disciplined, having Me as the highest. Because, he who has controlled his senses, his knowledge is established. BG2.61

2.13 Strive with discipline for Oneness, because for he who has controlled his senses, his knowledge is well-established.

Comment: This verse goes on by emphasizing that the wisdom obtained has to be applied in practice and that we have to strive on every level for Oneness in the large and the small, releasing attachments to the things we like or to the aversions we dislike. Then our knowledge becomes well-established.

For a man dwelling on the objects of the senses, attachment to them is born; from attachment, desire is born; from desire, anger is born; from anger comes delusion; from delusion, wandering of memory; from loss of memory, destruction of the intelligence; from destruction of the intelligence, he is lost. BG2.62/63

2.14 For he who dwells on the objects of the senses, attachment to them is born; from attachment, desire is born; from desire, anger is born; from anger, delusion; from delusion, confusion and destruction of the intelligence; and he is ruined.

Comment: In testing and applying obtained knowledge of the surrounding world, we should try to stay unattached. We should not become vain by the beauty of the confirmations and the applicability of our knowledge. Let us never stop testing and learning, so that our knowledge becomes applied knowledge, becomes wisdom. Attachments to the subtle objects of the senses are more difficult to release than attachments to the more obvious objects of the senses. If we do not go on imperturbably, we can once more become imprisoned by the objects of the senses and lose ourselves again.

But freed from desire and aversion, moving the objects of the senses with the senses, the self [that is] to be used by [means of] the restraints of the Self, attains stillness. BG2.64
For him, in stillness the abandonment of all sorrows is born; because, the intelligence of one whose mind is still becomes quickly stable. BG2.65

2.15 But he who is restrained by the Self, who treats the objects of the senses with the senses, freed from desire and aversion, attains peace by the urging of the self. Then his intelligence attains equanimity.

Comment: Treating the objects of the senses with the senses is to judge everything on its own merits without aversion or desire. This is attained by restraining the motions of the mind, the thinker in ourselves, the self with the help of the Self. Then Oneness is seen everywhere in good and in evil, and peace is attained. In learning this, our intelligence attains equanimity.

There is no intelligence for the [one who is] undisciplined, [there is] for the undisciplined no meditation, and [there is] for the non-meditating one no peace. Whence is the happiness for one who is without peace? BG2.66

Indeed, when the mind follows the wandering senses then it carries away one's knowledge like the wind a ship on water. BG2.67

2.16 He who does not strive for Oneness has no intelligence, and finds neither meditation or peace. He who has no peace does not know happiness. The mind follows the wandering senses and diverts his knowledge.

Comment: Using our intelligence, we can find out that Oneness is inevitable. Oneness means All, and not All and 'I'. Striving for Oneness and still holding onto the 'I' is not striving for Oneness. It leads to separation, and the intelligence is deluded by the ever-changing 'I', and real silence, living the ISness of Life, is missed. Then we do not come to meditation or to peace. Holding onto the 'I', the mind will follow the wandering senses, and the knowledge that Oneness is everywhere and that no separation is possible is gone. This will bring no peace or restraint of the self by the Self.

In that which [is] the night for all beings, the restrained one is awake; in which the beings are awake, that [is] the night for the hermit who sees. BG2.69

2.17 In that which is the night of all beings, he who restrains himself is awake; that in which the beings are awake is the night of the sage who sees.

Comment: The sage knows life and understands the nature of Life, not yet discovered or remembered by all beings. This ignorance of the nature of Life is the night for all beings. The wise one restrains himself, and what all beings find most important and chase after, the wise one sees has no use, due to his superior knowledge.

Abandoning all desires, the man who moves free from desire, without 'my-ness' and 'I-making', that one attains peace. BG2.71

2.18 He who is without 'I-making' (separateness) attains peace.

Comment: To separate ourselves from a particular side of life is not wise. Even, while knowing better, the wise also ought to learn from the wrongdoings of those who do not yet know. To separate ourselves from that is also 'I-ness' and does not bring peace. All is All and nothing is excluded. This is hard to learn, but the wise one knows that the wrongdoings of those who are ignorant bring *him* to reflection.

3 Striving for Oneness by action

In this world is a twofold state from old times on taught by Me, Arjuna, [one] by the yoga of knowledge of the followers of Sāṃkhya, [and one] by the yoga of action of yogis. BG3.3

3.1 The world is a twofold path: striving for Oneness by knowledge of the Philosophical System, and striving for Oneness by the action of strivers for Oneness.

Comment: The twofold path is the path that combines thinking and doing, knowledge and action, cause and effect, theory and practice, introvert and extrovert actions. Using the mind without applying knowledge is one-sided, just as action without knowledge or understanding is one-sided. Recognizing these opposites, this twofold path of thinking and doing, doing and thinking, while assimilating and balancing them in awareness of the difference, yields applied understanding and wisdom. The twofold path is always in motion due to the continuous change in experience by the process of assimilating the differences perceived.

Not from not initiating actions does man become free from action, nor from mere renunciation does he attain perfection. BG3.4

3.2 Man does not become free from acting by <u>not</u> undertaking actions, nor does he attain perfection by mere renunciation.

Comment: Gaining experience is to understand cause and effect. That understanding results in new differences that force action. Not acting due to laziness or fear does not give right results. The wish to avoid an act is confirmation that the act is needed. This is incorrect. On the other hand, a well-thought-out abstention of action is an active experience of cause and effect. Renunciation gives the experience of 'not wishing to do and is likewise only acceptable if it is performed as an inevitable, responsible experience in cause and effect.

For no one ever remains, even for a moment, without taking action; for unwillingly, every act is made to be done by the gunas born from the Primordial Substance. BG3.5

3.3 For no one ever remains, even for a moment, without taking action; for even unwillingly, everyone is forced to action by the Basic Attributes born from the Primordial Substance.

Comment: Life itself forces actions and man acts both consciously and unconsciously. The body needs air and food, and interrelates with the earth and all other beings. Non-action or giving up action is not possible. Even thinking a thought is action. So live life and take the inevitable actions.

[Although] restraining the organs of action, he who sits with his thoughts thinking on the objects of the senses, is self-deluded and called a hypocrite. BG3.6

3.4 He is a hypocrite who, although he restrains his organs of action, remains with his thoughts on the objects of the senses.

Comment: By having thoughts the action of thinking is performed, and in this case the passions, the objects of the senses, are followed in thought. This is action, and one deludes himself if the thought is not restrained while restraining the organs of the actions.

You perform regulated action; for action is better than non-action. And, even the maintenance of your body does not result from not acting. BG3.8

3.5 Complete the inevitable action. Action is better than non-action. The maintenance of your body would not even be possible without action.

Comment: An inevitable action is an action which, irrespective of the effect on the actor, has to be done, whether or not the actor likes or dislikes the result. The body asks for all kinds of actions for its maintenance. If necessary, it can act to produce a fever, uncomfortable for the person concerned, but ultimately beneficial for the whole body. We often do not look forward to inevitable actions that might arise from unpleasant situations in relationships, but we still have to act to balance that. If the situation is a pleasure, then we have no problem in taking right action.

Apart from action for the sake of sacrifice, this world is a bond to action; action with that motive, Arjuna, you perform free from attachment! BG3.9

3.6 This world is bound by action in action.

Comment: The law of cause and effect: the effect of an action will be the cause of another action. Simply do the inevitable action without labelling it with your limited personal view.

Know [that] action is coming from Brahman, Brahman being the source of the imperishable! Therefore, the omnipresent Brahman is constantly established in sacrifice. BG3.15

3.7 Know that action originates in THAT and THAT is imperishable. THAT is inevitably all-pervading and omnipresent.

Comment: Cause and effect are distinctions in THAT and action originates in the law of cause and effect. THAT is imperishable and expresses the inevitable unity of the motion of Life. In assimilation of the difference, by performing an action, the distinction is reflected in the unity of both opposites. In the cause, the effect is incorporated and vice versa. The law of cause and effect, as the manifestation of Life, is all-pervading and omnipresent.

Thus, he who does not cause to turn the rotated wheel here in this world, [he who is] malignant, [he whose] pleasure is in the sense[s], he lives in vain, Arjuna. BG3.16

3.8 Therefore, one who does not turn the rotating wheel and learn to restrain action lives in vain.

Comment: It is vain to oppose the general law of cause and effect. We can learn to apply and to restrain ourselves in action while following the law of cause and effect. Then there is no opposition to the movement of Life.

But the human being who takes pleasure in the Self alone, who should be satisfied and content only in the Self, for him there is nothing to do. BG3.17

3.9 The human being who takes pleasure in the Self alone, who is satisfied in the Self and contented only in the Self, for him there is nothing to do.

Comment: He who applies the law of cause and effect, without adding to or disturbing it, but lives fully the wholeness of Life, being in the Self, for him there are no worries about the course and movement of Life. The flow of Life is with and within him and there is nothing to add, to remove or to do, to change the flow of cause and effect. He is aware, alert, pouring his whole being into every moment. He is then in the Self and content in the Self.

For him there is even no purpose in what is done or not done here in this world, and his purpose is not depending on any being at all. BG3.18

3.10 He is not influenced by things to be done or not to be done. His interest does not depend on any being.

Comment: Living the wholeness of Life, going with the flow, moving with cause and effect, acting without residue, everything is at peace, in balance, and nothing else has to be done or not be done. Such a person is free and not attached to a particular, desired outcome. His attention is not fragmented, and he does not depend on any being, since he already lives every moment in wholeness and all beings are included.

Therefore, always perform the action that is to be done without attachment! Because, the man who is performing action without attachment attains the Supreme. BG3.19

3.11 Act without desire or attachment.

Comment: Do not perform incomplete fragmentary actions due to desires and attachments to particular outcomes. Such actions are one-sided and do not give the peace of actions rooted in wholeness.

For Me there is nothing, Arjuna, in the three worlds to be done, nor [anything] not attained to be attained; nevertheless I revolve around action. BG3.22

3.12 There is nothing in the three worlds to be done for THAT, nothing not attained that is to be attained; nevertheless THAT engages in action.

Comment: The manifestations in THAT of cause and effect, yielding reality, the three worlds: *past–present–future*, do not touch THAT, being whole, beyond space-time, manifesting space-time. Action would not be possible without THAT. In All-pervading THAT, All and Nothing simply IS.

These worlds would sink down if I did not act. I would be the creator of the intermixture confusion of castes and I would smite down these people. BG3.24

3.13 These worlds would perish if THAT did not act.

Comment: Space-time, cause and effect, is manifested by the action of limitation in THAT. Without these actions of THAT, the movement of Life in wholeness, these worlds would perish.

As the ignorant ones act attached in action, Arjuna, so the wise one should act without attachment, desirous of holding together the world. BG3.25

3.14 The ignorant ones act with attachment; the wise one however acts without attachment for the benefit of the world.

Comment: Those who are ignorant separate the 'I' from All and act with attachment to the 'I'. They do not share their beings in wholeness while imprinting their 'I' in the flow of life. The wise one does not separate the 'I' from All, does not see a separate you and 'I', only Oneness. The wise one lives the whole and shares his being quite naturally in the flow of Life without 'I-ness'. He is conscious of the effects of his acts in eternity and lives the wholeness for the benefit of the world.

By the gunas of the Primordial Substance, actions are being performed everywhere. Deluded by 'I-ness', the self thinks: 'I am the doer'. BG3.27

3.15 By the Basic Attributes of the Primordial Substance, actions are performed everywhere. Deluded by 'I-ness', the lower self thinks: 'I am the doer'.

Comment: When the Primordial Substance mirrors itself, actions, limitations, are performed in investigating the difference revealed in the triunity *manifest–difference–unmanifest*. The mind of the self, the thinker, mislead by the separation of the 'I' from the All, thinks: 'I am the doer', not seeing the wholeness and its echoes in the world. He is corrupting the Basic Attributes, the flow of cause and effect, with his 'I-ness'.

But Arjuna, he who knows the essence of the distinction between guna and action, thinking: 'The gunas revolve about the gunas', is not attached. BG3.28

3.16 He who knows the essence of the distinction between the Basic Attributes and actions, thinking: 'The Basic Attributes act on the Basic Attributes', is not attached.

Comment: Cause and effect is that everlasting operating force of nature, and when not disturbed by personally induced actions that are not part of a cause, then we are not attached, and the Basic Attributes act on the Basic Attributes. Since the effect is implied in the cause, we simply have to pass it on, according to the movement of Life in wholeness. The wise one is aware of this wholeness and will not disrupt the flow by 'I-actions', is not involved in fragmented actions, but pours his whole being into the moment of motion and has no attachment to 'I-ness' in the movement of Life.

Those who are deluded by a guna of the Primordial Substance are attached to the actions of the guna. The knower of the whole should not upset those foolish ones who know that what is not whole. BG3.29

3.17 Those who are deluded by the Basic Attributes of the Primordial Substance are attached to the actions of the Basic Attributes. Sages know the whole, ignorant ones do not know the whole.

Comment: He who wants to alter the flow of cause and effect by imposing his ambitions, thoughts, his 'I-ness', thinking that he is the doer, that he has to convert the cause into the effect according to his fragmented ideas, is attached to the actions of the Basic Attributes, and is deluded. The wise one will share his being in the wholeness of the movement of Life, not corrupting cause and effect by 'I-ambitions', knowing that 'I-ambitions' are not part of the cause that is already in the past and cannot be changed.

Depositing all actions in Me, with the mind on the essence of the Self, having become free from hope, selfishness and grief, fight! BG3.30

3.18 With your thoughts concentrated on the essence of the Self, fight, free from hope and selfishness, after your attachment has gone. THAT acts.

Comment: Fight with your thoughts in inner freedom while moving causelessly with the flow of Life, dying and rebirthing fully in every moment in the movement of Life. Perform only inevitable actions free from attachment to their results. We are easily distracted by personally induced actions, by not observing the whole, by being fragmented; we have to fight to release our selfishness. In understanding that everything IS already, the doubt implied in hope is not needed. While not revealing the unrevealed THAT, THAT acts in inevitable actions, the manifestations of THAT, expressing the law of cause and effect.

But [there are] those who, hairsplitting over this, do not practise My teaching, deluding all knowledge. Know them [as] lost [and] mindless! BG3.32

3.19 The hairsplitting over this teaching misleads all knowledge. The mindless ones are lost.

Comment: It is useless to discuss these teachings without applying them. We can witness the correctness of the teachings by their effectiveness. We need to follow the twofold path of theory and practice and balance any imbalances found. If we are only one-sided, then we are lost.

Even a wise one acts according his own nature. Beings follow their material nature. What will suppression accomplish? BG3.33

3.20 Wise ones are motivated by their own insights. Beings follow their nature.

Comment: We cannot copy or follow the thoughts of someone else without understanding and evaluating them and using our own insight. We should test these insights in practice, learn from the results in cause and effect, and correct them. Since the nature of each person is different, the results will be different. Our own insight should be sufficient to understand our deeds, but consider the deeds of others also with your insight and empathy to learn from them.

In the senses are situated desire for and aversion to the objects of the senses. One should not fall under the power of these two. Indeed, they are one's antagonists. BG3.34

3.21 In the senses are situated desire for and aversion to the objects of the senses. Let nobody come under the power of these two, since they are one's antagonists.

Comment: If we are not completely free, if there is even the slightest contamination of self-righteousness, of ego-motivation in our action, if the action is not a complete inevitable action following only the flow of cause and effect, effortless and causeless, then we are still under the power of desire and aversion rooted in conditions of the ego. We have to become aware of these conditions to let them go, otherwise they are or become our enemy.

Better the performance of one's own duty imperfectly than another's duty perfectly. Better death in one's own duty; [performing] another's duty brings danger. BG3.35

3.22 Better is death in one's own duty-of-life, though imperfect, than [doing] the duty-of-life of another; that is full of danger.

Comment: Even death is better than to adhere to the authority or instructions of others that are contrary to our own insights. It is better to live our own life with all its deficiencies and learn from the law of cause and effect to improve our own insights and behaviour by thinking and doing, by doing and thinking, than living under the instructions of authorities. Suppressing our own insights is like living in a mental straight-jacket.

In this regard, by what is this man impelled to commit evil, even unwillingly, Kṛṣṇa, as if urged by force? BG3.36

3.23 Why does man commit evil, even unwillingly, as if urged by force?

Comment: Unconstrained behaviour, or following emotions to come into possession of something or even someone, forces us to do what is regretted later on.

This desire, this anger, originates from the guna of Rajas. Know this all devouring great sin [to be] the enemy here! BG3.37

3.24 Desire, anger and annoyance originate from the Movement Power of the Basic Attributes.

Comment: The Movement Power, one of the three powers [Equilibrium, Movement, Perseverance], stands here for the imagination, the wrong thinking resulting in the emotions of desire, anger and annoyance.

Wisdom is enveloped by this eternal enemy of the wise: the protean, Arjuna, and an insatiable fire. BG3.39

3.25 Wisdom is enveloped by this eternal enemy of the wise: desire, an insatiable fire.

Comment: Desire, the belief that the ISness of Life is not lived, is an insatiable fire. After having restrained material desires, spiritual desires should be restrained. In the ISness, the wholeness of Life, All IS and there is nothing to desire.

The senses, the mind and the intelligence are called its seat; by means of these it causes confusion, obscuring the knowledge of the embodied one. BG3.40

3.26 The abode is the senses, the inner sense (Manas), and the intelligence; these cause wandering.

Comment: Be sensitive and alert that your intelligence in thinking is not covered by personal desires. Even doing good because we want to and not as a result of an inevitable action without 'I-ness', is wrongdoing.

Therefore, Arjuna, first control your senses and kill this very sin destroying [higher] knowledge and worldly knowledge! BG3.41

3.27 Control the senses and this destroyer of knowledge and science, this bondage to substance.

Comment: If the senses are not controlled, desires of all kinds can come up leading to attachments that disturb the flow of life, the knowledge of wholeness, and the awareness of its diversity.

They say: the senses are great; the mind is greater than the senses; the intelligence is greater indeed than the mind; but what is beyond the intelligence is 'the THAT'. BG3.42

3.28 The senses are great; greater is the inner sense; still greater the intelligence; the greatest is 'the THAT'.

Comment: This verse reminds us that to control the senses is a first step, restraining the mind is greater, while the subtle intelligence is still greater, but for the human being the highest possible is 'the THAT', which is the manifestation of what is all-permeating and unrevealed. All three levels of realization have to be restrained to open us to 'the THAT'.

Thus having known what is greater than the intelligence, having immobilized the self by the Self, slay the enemy, Arjuna, that difficult to assail protean! BG3.43

3.29 THAT is greater than the intelligence, restrains the self by the Self, and kills desire.

Comment: In the imperishable, all-pervading, unlimited THAT, the Oneness of the manifest and unmanifest, no 'I-ness' is possible. Then there is no desire, it is killed, and the thinker, the self, is constrained by the THAT, the Self, as a natural consequence.

4 Striving for Oneness by knowledge

I proclaimed this imperishable Yoga to the Sun God, the Sun God told [it] to Manu; Manu told [it] to the Son of Manu. BG4.1

4.1 This imperishable striving for Oneness I proclaimed to the Sungod, the Sungod to the Root-Manu, and the Root-Manu to the Seed-Manu.

Comment: Code language: Root and Seed generate each other. They are the same, both are Manu, each other's opposite. Both opposites generate each other in the difference, which shines forth as the Sungod, the shining awareness of realization in the triunity *Root-Manu–Sun God–Seed-Manu*. This triunity is beyond space-time in Oneness. The difference and the opposites have in their unity the imperishable striving for Oneness for him who seeks by applied knowledge and understanding. Oneness is coded by 'I'.

Thus the royal sages knew this [by] the lineage which was received. In this world, over a great period of time, this Yoga has vanished, Arjuna. BG4.2
Indeed this, this ancient Yoga, is proclaimed by Me to you today, since you are devoted and My friend. Certainly this is the highest secret. BG4.3

4.2 This striving for Oneness has vanished in a long lapse of time. Yet it is the highest secret.

Comment: By personalizing the code language in verse one, the impersonal truth has been lost in the passing of time. Please do see the kernel, the secret, the imperishable inevitable movement of assimilating the difference of *manifest–unmanifest*, that striving for Oneness without revealing the unrevealed One.

Many are my births and yours [that have] gone by, Arjuna. I know them all; you do not know [them], Arjuna. BG4.5

4.3 'The THAT' knows its births; you don't.

Comment: 'The THAT': the imperishable Self. The Self being imperishable is impersonal, not knowing life and death as separate, since the Self holds both. By fearing death we do not live life fully, and we do not remember the births of our incorrect insights as the Self does.

Even as I am unborn, being the imperishable Self, Lord of beings, yet being My own Material Nature, controlling Myself, I come into being by [My] own creative power. BG4.6

4.4 'The THAT' is unborn, the imperishable Self, the originator of the beings, although THAT controls itself and the Primordial Substance brings forth birth by the power of Māyā.

Comment: THAT is impersonal, all-pervading, unrevealed. In constraining itself, the personal 'the THAT', the reflection in THAT, unborn, expresses the ISness of THAT. It simply IS, without birth. In manifestation the imperishable Self originates the beings, by causing limitations in the manifestation-possibility: the Primordial Substance. Reality [Māyā] is born, is real, but is still an ongoing reflection [Māyā] of the movement of Life, the assimilation of the differences: the power of Māyā gives birth in the Changeful Changeless.

For whenever there is weakening of duty, Arjuna, the rising up of lawlessness, then I emit Myself. BG4.7
For the protection of the good and the destruction of evil doers, for the purpose of establishing duty, I come into being age after age. BG4.8

4.5 Whenever there is weakening of duty and rising up of lawlessness, then THAT manifests itself in sacrifice by embodiment, in age after age.

Comment: THAT is All; it adjusts, assimilates in manifestation, in embodiment. Breaking the Oneness of Life, the balance of Spirit and Substance, then THAT as cause and effect will always, age after age, show the consequences of the weakening of duty and rising up of lawlessness. Depleting the earth, exhausting oneself, ruining oneself, exploiting one's genius, burning the candle at both ends, are all examples of improper balance in Spirit and Substance. THAT embodies itself in the law of cause and effect and the results of egoistic behaviour will result in fragmentary living.

The one who does know My divine birth and action thus in essence, having abandoned the body, does not go to rebirth; he goes to Me, Arjuna. BG4.9
Many are those who, freed from passion, fear and anger, made of Me, relying upon Me, purified through the austerity of knowledge, come into My state of being. BG4.10

4.6 He who knows the agency as thus in truth is free from rebirth, nascent in the One.

Comment: One, knowing the action of THAT to live life in the harmony of Spirit and Substance without any need to emphasize them, will reside in the middle and become balanced, discovering what we are already: One.

In whatever way they attain Me, even so I participate in them. Human beings always follow My path, Arjuna. BG4.11

4.7 In whatever way human beings experience THAT, even so they themselves become THAT-conscious. Human beings inevitably follow the Path.

Comment: Since THAT is manifested in the law of cause and effect, everyone has to follow this law and will become conscious of the consequences of their actions, of their manifestations. Coming into this world, human beings have to follow their path of learning and responsibility, which leads inevitably to the Path of understanding, irrespective of the time needed.

Desiring the success of action, they offer to the gods in this world; indeed, in the human world, success is the direct result of action. BG4.12

4.8 In the human world, success results from action.

Comment: In manifesting oneself within one's manifested limitation, we have the power to harvest the effects of their causes by following THAT unattached.

The system of four castes was created by Me according to the distinction of the Basic Attribute and action. Know Me, of this the creator, likewise as non-acting and changeless! BG4.13

4.9 The realizations of THAT create birth-states according to the distinction of the Basic Attributes and actions, though non-acting and changeless.

Comment: Being conscious implies the creation of space-time. It implies therefore also the birth of the flow of cause and effect according to the awareness of the Basic Attributes: Perseverance

Power, Equilibrium Power, and Movement Power [14.2/BG14.5]. Imbalances in holding to perseverance or to movement are birth-states that can lead to insights on how to balance the imbalances in life and be in equilibrium. All this will not have an impact on THAT. As the law of cause and effect, THAT is not touched by its application and remains non-acting.

Actions do not taint Me, nor do I have desire for the fruits of action. He who knows Me thus is not bound by actions. BG4.14

4.10 Actions do not taint THAT, nor does THAT have desire for the fruit of the action. He who knows THAT thus is not bound by action.

Comment: The law of cause and effect is not tainted by the flow of actions occurring nor is any outcome desired; the law simply applies to every action. We should not interfere with the flow of Life by adding our desires, which is nothing more than doubting All IS, the ISness of Life. Simply do what is needed in the flow. Let us not disturb the flow and let us act in love and empathy without being bound to an expected outcome of our actions. We have to be restrained and disciplined in considering and accepting that in All IS, all is there to be manifested, for which we have to do our part.

Having known thus, action was performed also by the ancients, by those striving after liberation. So therefore, you perform action [as] previously performed by the ancients! BG4.15

4.11 Complete an action, desiring liberation.

Comment: Performing and completing an action while living in THAT gives release and peace.

What is action? What is non-action? Thus, even the sages are confused in this case. I shall explain that action to you. Knowing which, you shall be freed from harm. BG4.16

4.12 What is action? What is non-action? Even the sages are not sure of this. See here the explanation of action. This knowledge brings action.

Comment: The law of cause and effect is always working. An action results in a cause-and-effect sequence, while non-action results in a different cause-and-effect sequence. As action and non-action both have results, it is uncertain as to what is action and what is non-action. As THAT is always manifested in cause and effect, the sages know that cause and effect is constantly present, which includes action as well as the action implied in non-action. This knowledge releases the peace of performing action and non-action in a proper way.

One must know action, and also improper action and non-action. The way of action is hard to comprehend. BG4.17

4.13 Because one must know action, one must know improper action, and one must know non-action. The way of action is hard to comprehend.

Comment: It is difficult to learn to appreciate the cause of the effect, particularly for improper actions, because we might not like the effect. However, it is also an opportunity to learn for the better. So as not to disturb the flow of Life, expressed in cause and effect, we need to know about action, improper action, and non-action.

He who sees non-action in action and action in non-action, who is wise among men; he is disciplined, performing the complete act. BG4.18

4.14 He who sees in action non-action and in non-action action, he attains the knowledge of realization and strives for Oneness and completes his work.

Comment: In the flow of the ISness of Life, the ongoing sequences of cause and effect should not be disturbed by personal additions or omissions. Manyness goes over into Oneness, and is passed on by the observer into manyness again (see Figure 2.1). If done by assimilating the differences observed in the manyness while being awakened in Oneness, the flow will be undisturbed and the entire work, consisting of inevitable actions and non-actions, will be performed. This work involves action in non-action and non-action in action. We are growing and striving for Oneness by attaining the knowledge of awakened realization of the differences involved.

He whose undertakings are all free of intentions from desire, whose deed is burned by the fire of knowledge, the wise call him a teacher. BG4.19

4.15 He whose actions are free of intentions from desire, whose deeds have been burned by the fire of knowledge, is called wise.

Comment: He who sees and performs his actions and non-actions only as inevitable parts of the manifestations in THAT, without limited personal intentions, lives the ISness of Life. Personally influenced deeds do not occur since they have already been burned by the fire of this knowledge. Such a person is called wise.

Having abandoned attachment to the fruit of action, always satisfied, independent, and even [when] engaged in action, indeed he does nothing. BG4.20
Free from desires, his thoughts and self restrained, all acquisition abandoned, performing only bodily action, he does not obtain sin. BG4.21
[The one who is] spontaneously satisfied with what one obtains, transcending the pairs-of-opposites, unselfish, indifferent to success and failure, even having acted, he is not bound. BG4.22

4.16 After restraining his thoughts and his self, his body inevitably performs actions without attachment to the results of actions, free from the pairs-of-opposites, not bound.

Comment: Performing actions in inevitability is like being a clear lens that focuses manyness into Oneness and again into manyness without distorting the flow of Life. To be in unity with Oneness, we have to restrain our thoughts and the self, the mind, so as not to interfere in the flow of Life. The wise one has no use for duality or for the fruits of actions, but remains unbounded in his growth into Oneness through experiences.

Knowing that, you shall not fall again into error, Arjuna; [this is the knowledge] by which you shall see all beings in the Self, in other words in Me. BG4.35
Even if you are of evils the worst of all evildoers, yet you shall cross over all distress with the boat of knowledge. BG4.36

4.17 In the boat of knowledge thou shalt cross over all evil and see all beings in the Self.

Comment: Knowledge implying understanding gives us the insight that All is reflected in everything and in everyone. Thus there is no division in the observer and the observed; they are both manifested by the limitation involved. Evil can be identified with fragmentation of life instead of sharing and striving for Oneness. Through knowledge all evil, all fragmentation, will come to an end and by assimilation of the observer and the observed into Oneness, the omnipresence of all beings is experienced in the Self. Then we will experience the manyness as Oneness in our Self, and the observer and the observed will be one.

As kindled fire reduces firewood to ashes, Arjuna, so the fire of knowledge reduces all actions to ashes. BG4.37
[He who is] ignorant, faithless and of doubting nature perishes. There is no happiness, neither this world nor hereafter, for [he who is] of a doubting nature. BG4.40

4.18 The fire of intelligence reduces action to ashes. The doubter perishes.

Comment: In living by this knowledge, there is no desire for the fruits of actions. All fruits, all desired results, have been reduced to ashes. The actions performed simply catalogue our experiences in the omnipresence of Life without separation from the All. This way, actions will reveal that what is there, yet unknown to us, into the manifest without revealing the unmanifest, leading to the growth of our field of experience, and of our wisdom. The doubter of this knowledge will not gain wisdom, or see or strive for Oneness.

Actions do not bind [the one] possessed of the Self, Arjuna, [whose] action has been laid aside [by] Yoga, [and whose] doubt is cut away [by] knowledge. BG4.41

4.19 Striving for Oneness makes man master of his actions.

Comment: In striving for Oneness, only the manifestation in THAT of the law of cause and effect can be followed by assimilation of the differences manifested into Oneness of the observer and the observed. This striving makes man inevitably master of his actions.

Therefore, having cut off with the sword of knowledge of the Self the ignorance born from doubt abiding in the heart, stand by Yoga! Rise, Arjuna! BG4.42

4.20 Knowledge gives purification and realization in the Self. Rise, be your Self.

Comment: Knowledge and understanding of the manifestation in THAT, living with the flow of Life while not disturbing cause and effect by attachments, leads to realization in the Self. Do not procrastinate, stand up, accept your heritage, be your Self now!

5 Striving for Oneness by renunciation of action

Renunciation and Yoga of action are the two makers of the highest bliss. But, of these two, Yoga of action is better than renunciation of action. BG5.2

5.1 Renunciation of action and striving for Oneness by action both provide the highest bliss. The second is better.

Comment: Relinquishment, renunciation of action implies that any fruit of action for one's own benefit is given up. The idea that the observed and the observer are independent from each other has been conquered. Striving for Oneness is the better choice. Then, not only is the law of cause and effect in an action fully understood and there are no longings for the results of an action, but also only those actions are performed that are inevitable and in cooperation with the whole.

He who neither hates nor desires, free from the pairs-of-opposites, is to be known as a perpetual renouncer. Indeed, Arjuna, he is easily liberated from bondage. BG5.3

5.2 Perpetual renunciation, without hate or desire, free from the pairs-of-opposites, gives liberation from bondages.

Comment: In understanding the triunity *observed–difference–observer*, the difference unites observer/observed and these are no longer considered as a pair of opposites. By assimilating the difference in the flow of Life, while not tainting the sequence of cause and effect with hate or desire, there is no obstacle to the growth towards experiencing the ISness of Life.

Children, rather than teachers, declare Sāṃkhya and Yoga [as] separate. The person who has performed either one of them correctly, obtains the fruit of both. BG5.4

5.3 Renunciation and striving for Oneness are distinctions; being unseparated, the practice of either one gives the fruit in the other.

Comment: Striving for Oneness implies renunciation and both as such are inseparable and so are the fruits of their practice.

The realm which is attained by Sāṃkhyans is also reached by yogis, and the person who sees Sāṃkhya and Yoga [as] one [truly] sees. BG5.5

5.4 Renunciation and striving for Oneness are one.

Comment: In practicing renunciation or relinquishment, the action performed is inevitable, since the actions are such that they do not disturb the flow of cause and effect. A wise one can perform only such actions, and those actions are then inevitable. However, in striving for Oneness, we are always conscious of the inevitability of the actions performed. The final result of both becomes in fact the same.

But renunciation, Arjuna, without Yoga is difficult to attain. The hermit disciplined in Yoga quickly attains Brahman. BG5.6

5.5 Striving for Oneness is difficult without renunciation.

Comment: As striving for Oneness implies renunciation, it is difficult to strive for Oneness without renunciation. Renunciation is advisable and necessary.

[The person who is] disciplined in yoga, whose Self has been purified, who has conquered the Self, subdued the senses, whose Self has become the Self of all beings, is not tainted even when acting. BG5.7

5.6 He whose goal is striving for Oneness, he whose Self has been purified, he who controls his Self and has subdued his senses, he whose Self has become the Self of all beings, is not bound.

Comment: The striver for Oneness, who is living the ISness of life, who understands that the observer and the observed are one, is limitless, unbounded, since he assimilates the manifested difference in the triunity *observed–difference–observer* without adding self-imposed restrictions and attachments. He has purified his Self by seeing the unity and omnipresence of each Self, so there cannot be any other Self than the Self of all beings in every being. His senses are subdued, restrained, although force or control are never needed in the ISness of Life.

Indeed, 'I do nothing', thus the disciplined knower of truth should think, when he is seeing, hearing, touching, smelling, eating, walking, sleeping, breathing, talking, defecating, grasping, even when opening and closing his eyes, while holding to [the idea]: 'The senses dwell among the objects of the senses'. BG5.8/9

5.7 'I do nothing!' the striver for Oneness should think, he who knows the truth, seeing, hearing, touching, smelling, standing, walking, sleeping, breathing. The senses dwell among the objects of the senses.

Comment: The striver for Oneness is active in not disturbing the flow of energies of the universe; it is not his doing, he is only following the ongoing dance of the energies of the universe, while maintaining his body in balance. So he is not directing, he is not doing, but only being active for living wholeness without attachments.

With the body, the mind, the intelligence, even with the senses alone, yogis undertake action for the purification of the Self, having abandoned attachment. BG5.11
[The person who is] disciplined, having abandoned the fruit of action, obtains final peace. [However, who is] undisciplined, attached to the fruit, is [spontaneously] bound by the action of a desire. BG5.12

5.8 With the body, with the mind, with the intelligence, and even with the senses alone, the strivers for Oneness undertake actions for the purification of the Self, after having abandoned attachment. This gives the peace of THAT.

Comment: Psychological involvements attached to the actions of the mind, of the senses, of the body, of the intelligence has to be abandoned, renounced. The feeling and thinking of 'I am the doer', that 'I-ness' has to leave for the purification of the Self, for living wholeness: the silence and peace of THAT.

Having renounced all actions with the mind, the embodied one is a happy ruler sitting in a nine-gated city, neither acting nor even causing action. BG5.13

5.9 After having renounced all actions in thought, the embodied one sits, as ruler within the nine-gated city, not bound.

Comment: Being full of action using his body, the nine-gated city [two eyes, two ears, two nostrils, one mouth, and the organs of generation and excretion], to perform the inevitable actions needed for letting the cosmic energies flow unbounded, he has renounced thoughts for actions bound to attachments, to psychological involvements. In living that wholeness, he is unbounded.

The Lord of the world emits neither agency nor acts nor the union of action and [its] fruit. Rather [its] inherent-self-nature sets [all] in motion. BG5.14

5.10 The Self of the world sends forth neither agency nor action nor the union of action and its fruit, but the inherent-self-nature urges.

Swabhava, inherent-self-nature, Changeful Changeless, the turning of the cosmos into itself searching for its own unlimitedness in limitedness, brings forth Life as ISness. There is no goal that has to be obtained by activities or actions or the results of actions.

The Lord admits neither the evil nor even the virtue of anyone. Knowledge is concealed by ignorance. By this, men are deluded. BG5.15

5.11 THAT accepts neither the evil, nor even the virtue, of anyone. Ignorance conceals knowledge.

Comment: The manifestations of THAT leaves THAT untouched. Ignorance is bound to manifestations and hence envelops knowledge.

But those whose ignorance of the Self is destroyed by the knowledge, their knowledge is like the sun, it illuminates THAT Supreme. BG5.16

5.12 But for those in whom this ignorance has been destroyed by the knowledge of the Self, for them the realization reveals THAT.

Comment: In releasing the limitations of the self, the mind and the sense of bonded 'I-ness', the silence of the unlimited Self becomes the friend of the self. This knowledge of the Self also touches the realization of THAT, not by holding it but by living its unlimited emptiness.

They whose thoughts are on THAT, whose Self is in 'THE', whose dedication is to 'THE', who are devoted to 'THE', go where there is no return, their sins removed by knowledge. BG5.17

5.13 Those whose thoughts are concentrated on THAT, whose Self is in 'THE', whose abode is in 'THE', whose refuge is in 'THE', go where there is no return.

Comment: By keeping the Self in 'THE', an utterance of the nameless emptiness that assimilates THIS and THAT unmanifested and unrevealed, there is no return to the night of ignorance, to the pairs-of-opposites, or to the belief of a thing-in-itself.

Pleasures, which are born out of contacts, indeed, are truly wombs of sorrow. They have a beginning and an end, Arjuna. The wise [one] does not take pleasure in them. BG5.22

5.14 Pleasures, which are born from contacts (separateness), are truly wombs of sorrow. They have a beginning and an end.

Comment: In the night of ignorance, chasing after pleasures is the expression of imbalance in the self and fortifies sorrow as its opposite. Both sorrow and pleasure are not lasting.

The seers, whose sins have been worn away, whose twofold states have been cut [away], whose selves are controlled, who are devoted to the welfare of all beings, attain the Nirvāṇa of Brahman. BG5.25

5.15 The Seers attain the peace of Nirvāṇa after their twoness has been destroyed and their self has been controlled.

Comment: Remain in the middle, in that silence and emptiness of the pairs-of-opposites, where the opposites have been assimilated. That silence is called the peace of Nirvāṇa.

[For those] whose selves are cognized the Nirvāṇa of Brahman is found in the presence of self-restrainers whose minds are subdued and detached from desire and anger. BG5.26

5.16 For self-restrainers, who have cast aside desire and anger and have subdued their thoughts, who have learnt to know the Self, the realization in THAT lies near.

Comment: For living the peace of Nirvāṇa in our life, it is a prerequisite not to be touched by desire and anger and to restrain our thoughts. In learning to trust the Self as the friend of our self, realization of the imperishable omniscient silence and emptiness is near.

6 Striving for Oneness by self-restraint

The one who is independent of the fruit of the action performs an action [that has] to be done, he is both a renouncer and a Yogi. Not he who is without fire and 'not-doing'. BG6.1

6.1 He who, independent of the fruit of the action, performs an action of which the inevitability is certain, is a renouncer and a striver for Oneness. Not so is he who is without the fire of action and is inactive.

Comment: While participating fully in daily life, a renunciant performs necessary actions that are complete without being psychologically attached to the results of the actions. The striver for Oneness is not only a renunciant, but performs all the inevitable actions that will strengthen the unity and wholeness of Life. No one can become a renunciant by doing nothing. Actions, independent of the fruit of the action, done in inevitability, are needed to harmonize Life.

Thus, what they call renunciation, know that as Yoga, Arjuna! For no one [who] has not renounced [his] intention is a Yogi. BG6.2

6.2 Renunciation is striving for Oneness. No one who has not renounced his intentions is a striver for Oneness.

Comment: Renunciation is implied by striving for Oneness. The striver for Oneness understands that everything is already there in the wholeness of Life and avoids distortions created from holding to 'I-ness' conclusions, which distort the flow of cause and effect. A fullfilled renunciation becomes striving for Oneness. This is the effect of the cause 'renunciation'. Therefore, striving for Oneness is more advanced than renunciation.

Action is said to be the means of the hermit desirous of attaining Yoga. For him [who] has attained Yoga, equanimity is said to be the means. BG6.3

6.3 Coming to striving for Oneness brings action. Striving for Oneness itself: peacefulness.

Comment: If, in the interplay of Life and the living, only actions are performed that are inevitable for the inseparable wholeness of both Life and living—without desires or attachments for the results of the ongoing flow of cause and effect—then peace is the natural result of the actions of striving for Oneness.

Let him uplift the self by the Self, let him not weight upon the self, for truly, the Self is the ally of the self; yet the Self is the enemy of the self. BG6.5

6.4 Let him uplift the self by the Self and do not let the self be depressed, for truly, the Self is the ally of the self; the Self is also the enemy of the self.

Comment: The self is filled with various depressing qualities, like fear, impatience, selfness, etc. If the self is active in overcoming these negative qualities, then the Self is the ally of the self, if the self holds to them, then the Self is the enemy of the self. The mind is occupied with the manyness and we are looking outside without seeing the inside, the insight of wholeness, Oneness, that All that we are: cosmic omniscient realization. By looking inside, the light of the Self will help to overcome the separateness of the self in its clinging to the manyness, the darkness of those who are ignorant. The inner driving force of the Self will be the enemy of the self if it holds to darkness. The Self is the inner drive to dissolve procrastination about taking the path to Oneness.

Where the self has been conquered by the Self, the Self is the ally of [that] self, but the Self would indeed remain, like an enemy, in enmity with the not-self. BG6.6

6.5 The Self is the ally of the self for those in whom the self has been conquered by the Self. The Self is however the enemy of the not-self.

Comment: In taking the path to Oneness, the Self is the friend of the self that shows an open mind. The Self is the enemy of the closed mind—that mind that is biased, that echoes the meanings of others, that is prejudiced without looking at the facts presented by cause and effect, or that is not open to other interpretations.

[He whose] self is satiated with [higher] knowledge and worldly knowledge, [who is] situated on the peak, [who has] conquered [his] senses, [who is] thus yoked, he is called a yogi. [For him] a clod, a stone and gold are the same. BG6.8

6.6 He who restrains the self and to whom all are equal is striving for Oneness.

Comment: 'I' here and the world there is not Oneness. In striving for Oneness, a necessary condition is the restraining of the self, that feeling of 'I-ness' and separateness shown in the unrestrained movements of the mind.

He who is impartial to friend, companion, and enemy, neutral among relatives, foes, and even of one mind concerning good and evil people, is superior. BG6.9

6.7 He is conscious of the differences.

Comment: Being conscious of the differences, we assimilate the differences in Oneness without distorting the flow of Life.

Let the Yogi constantly discipline the self, remaining in solitude, alone, restraining his mind and self, free from desires, without property. BG6.10

6.8 He is natural in the realization of his smallness and knowing little.

Comment: All IS Nothing, Nothing IS All: IS. In the limited, the unlimited is implied. By choosing a point of origin, space is defined. A droplet on a leaf reflects the environment. How much do we know of the manyness, where it comes from and reflects in its Oneness, and to which it returns? If we think that we know so much, we need to visit a library or look up at the sky to realize we don't.

Indeed, this is a Yoga of not eating too much, but not necessarily of not eating, and not [a Yoga] of the habit of excessive sleep, nor indeed of wakefulness, Arjuna. BG6.16

6.9 He is pure, concentrated in thought, sober and pure in food, not idle.

Comment: To perform the inevitable actions in the flow of cause and effect, the body and mind should be in balance and properly maintained.

This is Yoga of [one who is] disciplined in taking in and giving out, disciplined in actions and activity, disciplined in sleep and wakefulness. It is the destroyer of sorrow. BG6.17

6.10 He eats no meat, nor drinks fermented beverages.

Comment: Aside from the killing, in eating meat we have to digest also the thoughts, fears, and the anger of the animal. Vegetarian food is much more pure. Alcohol is not beneficial for concentrating our thoughts.

When the mind, restrained, abides in the Self alone, abstaining from for all desires, then it is thus called disciplined. BG6.18

6.11 Thus he strives for Oneness.

Comment: Being pure and moderate in eating, sleeping, and exercising for the maintenance of the body, being balanced, he performs inevitable actions to assimilate the differences in the movement of Life.

One should know that the dissolution of the union with sorrow is what is called Yoga. This Yoga is to be practised with determination, not with a downcast mind. BG6.23

6.12 Let it be known that the dissolution of the union with sorrow is what is called striving for Oneness.

Comment: This verse is an encouragement to become a striver for Oneness, since striving for Oneness dissolves sorrow.

Wherever the restless and unsteady mind wanders, restraining [it] in [all] those places, one should bring [it] under the power of the Self alone. BG6.26

6.13 Wherever the restless and unsteady mind wanders, one should constantly control it and bring it under the power of the Self.

Comment: Personally directed thoughts cannot participate while performing the inevitable actions in the movement of cause and effect. Therefore, to be a striver for Oneness, the movements of the mind should be restrained and controlled by the Self so that the wholeness of life is enjoyed.

Looking in every direction with impartial eyes, self-disciplined in Yoga, he sees the Self abiding in all beings, and all beings in the Self. BG6.29

6.14 He sees the Self abiding in all beings, and all beings abiding in the Self.

Comment: That omniscient energy of Life, the Self, manifested in THAT without revealing THAT, is present in all beings; although the beings limit themselves in thought. The Self is whole.

He who sees Me everywhere and sees all in Me, to him I am not lost, and he is not lost to Me. BG6.30

6.15 He who sees THAT everywhere and sees all in THAT, for him THAT is not lost, nor does he lose THAT.

Comment: He who sees that the manifestations of THAT are everywhere and understands that THAT pervades all, for him THAT IS; while he who is bound to the expressions of limitation sees only the limitation and loses THAT.

He who dwells in Oneness partakes of Me as I dwell in all beings. Even when he is turning in every direction that Yogi turns inside of Me. BG6.31

6.16 He lives in THAT and THAT in him.

Comment: He lives the Changeful Changeless seeing the movement of all the energies in unlimited space without a fixed point or centre; being the timeless Vastness without a goal, he IS, living in THAT with THAT in him.

Without doubt, Arjuna, the mind is difficult to restrain and unsteady, but by practice, Arjuna, and dispassion, it is restrained. BG6.35

6.17 The mind is difficult to restrain and unsteady, but steady practice restrains it.

Comment: The mind is attached, involved in the movements of all the energies from all the collected conditions and emotions of the past. By careful looking at those energies with non-involvement, studying them will restrain the mind and balance the energies. The steady practicing of concentration, meditation and contemplation will restrain the mind.

Truly, dear Arjuna, his destruction is found neither here below nor there above, for no one [who] acts virtuously goes to misfortune. BG6.40

6.18 Nobody who acts attuned to nature takes the Path-of-Sorrow. He will have numerous chances.

Comment: One who follows cause and effect without attachments, according to one's possibilities, will not end on the Path-of-Sorrow, although the lessons of life can be momentarily painful. Consider those lessons as a gift for learning. If we are still involved in and attached to the conditions of the past, life will repeat the lessons differently for our education. The understanding will be reflected in the re-embodiment.

He who has no free will is carried off by that prior practise alone. Indeed, he who even wishes to know of Yoga surpasses Vedic recitation. BG6.44

6.19 By prior practices, he is irresistibly carried away.

Comment: The conditions of the past are powerful and have to be released by non-attachment and non-involvement and with love for the whole, otherwise we are carried on the Path-of-Sorrow.

But the Yogi whose mind is restrained and who is fully purified of sin is, through his persevering effort, perfected through many births. Then he goes to the highest path. BG6.45
The Yogi is superior to the ascetics, is considered superior even to the gnostics, and [is] superior to the ritualists. Therefore, be a Yogi, Arjuna! BG6.46
He who, full of faith, partakes of Me with an inner Self that has come to Me, is in my opinion the most disciplined of all Yogis. BG6.47

6.20 The striver for Oneness, perfected through many births, striving with perseverance, goes to the highest goal: the coming into THAT with his inner Self.

Comment: Going through renunciation in striving for Oneness after purifying his mind, body, and being steadfast, the striver for Oneness understands that all manifestations in THAT are limitations to expressing the unlimited Self. If he has not yet overcome those limitations it is still a goal to strive for, although, being in the union of the Self with THAT, no goal can be found anymore.

7 Striving for Oneness by distinguished knowledge

I shall tell you in full this [higher] knowledge [together with] the faculty of discernment; knowing which [there] remains nothing else to be known here. BG7.2

7.1 The knowledge and wisdom shall be told to you in full; if you know this, nothing else remains to be known here.

Comment: The science of spirituality and the basic law of thinking is fully explained in the Gītā. Here, in this world, there is nothing more to be known, only to be applied.

One man among thousands strives for perfection. Even among those who strives for perfection [only] one knows Me in essence. BG7.3

7.2 Among a thousand men, hardly one strives for perfection. Even among strivers who have reached perfection, hardly one knows THAT in essence.

Comment: Being busy with daily life, not many people study the science of spirituality and strive for Oneness. In its simplicity it is difficult to comprehend, and only a few people know THAT in essence.

Earth, water, fire, air, ether, mind, intelligence and even 'I-ness'; this, My eightfold Material nature, is thus divided. BG7.4

7.3 Earth, water, fire, air, ether, mind, intelligence and 'I-ness': that is the eightfold divided nature of the World.

Comment: Code language: The sphere of *water–fire* envelops the planet and perpendicular to that is the field of *earth–air*. Those four fields express all material properties and possibilities of the earth. This is the Substance part of the nature of the World. The spiritual part is given in the pairs-of-opposites of *air–ether, fire–mind, water–intelligence*, and *earth–'I-ness'*. The movements of the mind are also seen in fire, intelligence's unlimited possibility of dissolving everything in understanding, just as water dissolves everything; the intangibility of thought-ether is often like air turbulence, and the bondage of 'I-ness' is mirrored in the solidification of the earth.

This [is] the non-transcendent in this world, know [that there is] another, [which is] My transcendent Material nature: the substance of Life, Arjuna, by which this world is supported! BG7.5

7.4 This is the lowest. Know that there is also another nature of the World: the substance of Life.

Comment: The assimilation of the differences expressed in the opposites of the previous verse is the Substance part of the nature of the World. Expressed in pairs-of-opposites, the spiritual part of Substance is the Life-element, without giving the eightfold specification. The lowest implies the highest in the distinction of the difference. In the assimilation of the difference, there is no preference for high or low.

Thus look at all the beings, these forms of existence! I [am] the origin and likewise the dissolution of the whole world. BG7.6

7.5 These are the two wombs of all beings. It is the Origin as well as the Dissolution.

Comment: There is one law, here told in full: as above, so below. All beings live the difference as the manifest, but without revealing Substance unmanifest or Spirit unmanifest, here uttered as Origin and Dissolution, and hinted at in the verses 7.3/4.

And those states of being which are Sattvic as well as those partaking Rajas and Tamas, know them to be from Me alone, I am not in them; rather, they are in Me! BG7.12

7.6 Know that the natures, which are of the Equilibrium Power, the Movement Power, and the Perseverance Power, are from THAT; but not THAT in them, they in THAT.

Comment: The ongoing movement of manyness into Oneness into manyness again is also expressed in the attributes: Equilibrium Power, the living in the Now; Movement Power, the projection into the future; and Perseverance Power, the holding to the past. These attributes are also qualities that can be coupled to the behaviour of beings as manifestations in THAT.

This whole world is deluded by these three gunas generated states of being. It does not know Me as higher than these [and] imperishable. BG7.13

7.7 By these natures, which arise from the Three Basic Attributes, this whole world is deluded and does not know THAT, which is above it and imperishable.

Comment: Bound by the movements of time, the ongoing movement of *was–is–will be*, we do not realize that these movements are the manifestations in THAT of conversions of the energies, without revealing the imperishable THAT.

For this divine illusion of Me, produced by the guna, is difficult to comprehend. Only those who resort to Me overcome this illusion. BG7.14

7.8 Now this illusion, produced by the Basic Attributes, is difficult to comprehend. By the realization of 'THE', this illusion becomes understandable.

Comment: In 'THE', the dissolution in the assimilation of the difference in the pairs-of-opposites *THIS–THAT*, both imperishable omniscient unmanifested, there is no eternity, no time, only profound fathomless Vastness. In the realization of 'THE', the process of the re-choice of limitations creating space-time becomes understandable as manifestations in THAT, which are our seeming reality.

At the end of many births, the wise one resorts to Me. Vāsudeva [is] all!, 'the THAT', the very difficult to find great soul. BG7.19

7.9 At the end of many births, he who possesses wisdom comes to dissolution in THAT.

Comment: Wisdom as applied knowledge and understanding is obtained only after many deaths. Gaining wisdom, we come to dissolution in THAT to express Oneness, that love, either in this world or beyond.

Those whose knowledge has been carried away by these desires resort to other gods, practising all kinds of rites, constrained by their own material nature. BG7.20

7.10 Those whose knowledge has been carried away by desire resort to gods and follow all kind of rites by their obfuscation of the knowledge constrained by their nature.

Comment: This verse can be illustrated by a short story I once read in which a landscape is divided into two parts by a ravine. One side is covered with beautiful, small blue flowers, and a bright shining figure is noticed in the far distance. On the other dark rocky side, there are only a few unnoticed flowers and the people gathered are asking in all kinds of rites for the light to come over to them. Obviously they do not understand that they have to build a bridge or that they have only to fill up the ravine of their ignorance to cross over to the light. They do not understand that their desire, driven by personal motive is finite, is a form of separateness distorting the flow of life that results from the cause and effect of inevitable actions.

But finite [is] their fruit that is [for those] of little intelligence. They come to worshipping the gods, indeed, My devotees come to Me. BG7.23

7.11 However, the fruits of desire for God, rites and ceremonies that adhere to those of little intelligence, are finite.

Comment: The selfish separateness of the desire for God is finite since one looks outside. One creates a separate 'I', and 'non-I' called God. One denies the wholeness that we are by performing rites and ceremonies, not understanding that creator and creation are the same.

The unintelligent ones believe of Me [as] the unmanifest entered manifestation, not knowing My supreme, imperishable, highest nature. BG7.24

7.12 The unintelligent ones believe that THAT, the unmanifest, has come to manifestion, as they do not know of the supreme, imperishable, and highest nature.

Comment: Believing and entering into manifestation is accepting a beginning, which implies an ending. This denies the eternity and as a consequence the imperishable and indestructible nature is lost.

I am not visible to all [who are] enveloped in Māyā Yoga. This deluded world does not know Me, the unborn, the imperishable. BG7.25

7.13 THAT is not observable to all who are enveloped in the Māyā of striving for Oneness. This world does not know THAT, the unborn, the imperishable.

Comment: Even in the reality of performing Oneness, the illusion remains of subject and object. Observable are limitations, so THAT is not knowable, is unborn, imperishable. Still it is possible to live the unlimited THAT, without a beginning and an ending.

I know the beings of the past, present and future, Arjuna, but no one knows Me. BG7.26

7.14 THAT knows the things of the past, present and future, but THAT is not known by anyone.

Comment: Time is the realization, the setting of a limitation, a point in the eternal movement of the ongoing Now creating a before and an after. Nothing is created, only manifested in THAT, and THAT is untouched and undivided by the realization of differences. THAT is impossible to be known by us, since we can only perceive differences as a result of limitation.

By the delusion of the pairs-of-opposites, Arjuna, arising from desire and aversion, all beings fall into delusion at birth, Arjuna. BG7.27

7.15 By the delusion of the pairs-of-opposites, arising from attraction and aversion, all beings fall into delusion at their birth.

Comment: We name and create pairs-of-opposites, not realizing that the opposites become one in their difference. Therefore, desire implies aversion and vice versa. Without assimilation of the difference into Oneness, that simultaneity in ISness, all beings are torn between pairs-of-opposites and fall into delusion.

They who know Me as the essence of the material objects and the essence operating in the material objects, and as the essence of sacrifice, they know Me even at the time of death, [their] minds disciplined. BG7.30

7.16 They who know THAT as one with the essence of the elements, and the essence of the beings as one with the essence of action, are wise.

Comment: All separation is taken away in this verse. Our actions mirror the unmanifest in the interaction of the energies of the cosmos, expressing the Oneness as manyness, and the manyness as Oneness, being whole during these processes, expressing the ISness of Life. Our actions follow the whole in all its manifestations and are not loaded with attachments; our actions and THAT are united.

8 Striving for Oneness to the imperishable THAT

Kṛṣṇa, what is this Brahman? What is the essence of the Self? What is action? What is told of the essence of the material objects? What is said of the essence operating in the material objects? BG8.1

8.1 What is that 'THE'? What is the essence of the Self? What is action? What is the essence of the elements? What is the essence of the beings?

Comment: Never stop asking: 'What is THAT?' with an open mind, unbiased.

Kṛṣṇa, how and what is the essence of sacrifice here in this body? And how are you to be known by the self-controlled ones at the time of death? BG8.2

8.2 How and what is the essence of action here in this body? How can those who are controlled by the self know THAT?

Comment: Seven essential questions to understand the cosmos and its manifestations for self-awareness raised in this and the previous verse are fully discussed in the Gītā. As an exercise: try to answer these questions yourself first; meditate on them.

Brahman is the imperishable, the highest. The essence of the Self is called the inherent-self-nature. The nature of beings, the creative force, causer of creation, is called action. BG8.3

8.3 THAT is the imperishable, the highest. The inherent-self-nature is understood as the essence of the Self, the radiance that causes procreation and development of the beings, called inevitable action.

Comment: THAT is called the highest from our limited viewpoint, but no qualities can be given to the sublime imperishable nature, where there is neither highest or lowest. In that mutually inclusive interplay of All and Nothing, that interplay of the manifested and the unmanifested, that Changeful Changeless, that urge of self-awareness of the cosmos, is expressed its inherent-self-nature, holding the manifest as One with the unmanifest in inevitable action, the cycling movement of *manyness–Oneness–manyness*.

The essence of the material objects is the perishable nature, and the Supreme Spirit is the essence operating in the material objects. Indeed, I am the essence of sacrifice here in the body, Arjuna. BG8.4

8.4 The essence of the elements is the perishable nature, and the Primordial Spirit is the essence of the beings. The essence of action is in the body.

Comment: Spirit and Substance are mutually inclusive as is the interaction of the imperishable and perishable. The expression of the Spirit as the essence of the beings is in the action of pouring our whole being into every interplay, into every relationship. Then the essence of action is in that condensed cosmos, the body.

Let him remember the wise, the ancient, the ruler, smaller than the small, of all the bearer of unthinkable form; the radiance of the Sun beyond the darkness; at the time of death with steady mind, with dedication, endowed with Yoga power, the vital breath entering in the space between the eyebrows, thus at the same time he approaches that divine Supreme Spirit, which the knowers of the Veda call the imperishable, which the self-restrainers enter; they live desiring a life of chastity free from attachments, that path I shall declare to you briefly. BG8.9–11

8.5 Think of the wise, the ancient, the ruler, smaller than the small, of all the bearer of unthinkable form; of the radiance of the Sun beyond the darkness. Think with dedication and will of the Oneness, with power to strive for Oneness, and thus come to the realization of the Primordial Spirit, the imperishable, the Path of liberated self-restrainers.

Comment: This verse is a beautiful echo of 'THE'. The infinitesimally small implies the infinitely large, forms unthinkable beyond our cosmos, that light of bliss beyond light, light that implies darkness. By pouring their whole being into that Oneness in full holistic dedication to it, and by performing totally unattached inevitable actions, self-restrainers follow the Path to the awareness of the imperishable Primordial Spirit.

Thus he who dies, uttering Om, the monosyllable Brahman, remembering Me, leaving the body, he attains the highest goal. BG8.13

8.6 When the life's will is focused in the creative order of matters in thinking, in everything resonating with the same vibration of inevitability, one attains the highest goal (no re-embodiment).

Comment: In thinking, in the re-choices of limitations, that vibration of the condensed life-will, space-time realization is expressed while eternity is mirrored in All. By not burdening that accord of life with the dissonants of attachments, the flow of life is in harmony with its inevitable actions, and there is no need for re-embodiment. Those controlled by the self do not know that in ISness there is no goal, no purpose..

From the unmanifest all the manifestations come forth at the beginning of the day, they dissolve at the beginning of the night in that same one, known as the unmanifest. BG8.18

8.7 From the unmanifest, the manifest comes forth in inevitable action, but also comes to dissolution, all in due time.

Comment: The limitation still found in the unmanifest with the manifest as pairs-of-opposites is released from its time bondage. The unmanifest is deepened and freed by being represented as the state of the assimilated difference of *manifest–dissolution*, the eternal flow from form into formless, and from formless into form, without revealing itself. The verse gives utterance to the unmanifest, although it cannot be named or revealed.

But higher from that state is another unmanifest from the primaeval unmanifest, that which, when all beings perish, does not perish. This unmanifest is imperishable, thus it is said. They call it the highest goal; when attaining it, they return. That is My supreme abode. BG8.20/21

8.8 However, THAT is unmanifest and imperishable. THAT is said to be the highest goal.

Comment: The unmanifest is not touched by the ongoing flow of the reciprocal creation of form and formless; it simply IS, imperishable. Expressing time realization, it is called the highest goal, although in eternity and in imperishability no goal can be found.

Fire, light, day, the bright lunar fortnight, the six months of the northern path of the sun; passing away then, the men who know Brahman go to Brahman. Smoke, night, thus the dark six month of the southern path of the sun; the Yogi attaining the moonlight then returns. BG8.24/25
For these two paths of the world, light and dark, are considered as eternal. By one he goes for non-return, by the other he returns again. BG8.26

8.9 The striver for Oneness learns to know two paths: the light and the grey path. The first one knows no return; the second one bestows the lunar light and return.

Comment: The moon only partly reflects the light of the sun, the source of light. Always go to the source. Drinking the bright light of understanding will not blind you. Once understood, there is no return to ignorance and birth, pictured as the grey path. The light of the moon gives only a faint reflection of the source. The essence, the truth found in the source, has been absorbed by the moon, forcing a rebirth and a return to the source for understanding. That return can be stimulated by the lunar light clearly seen in the darkness of the night [ignorance].

9 Striving for Oneness by science and wisdom

But this most secret [teaching] I shall declare to you, to the not envious one: [higher] knowledge and worldly knowledge combined, knowing which you shall be liberated from evil. BG9.1

9.1 Science and wisdom of the secret teaching together give liberation from evil.

Comment: The echo of the universe reflected in our thinking, via science and wisdom, that applied knowledge and understanding, is called secret, as the process of the assimilation of differences is not seen or comprehended. However, that process is available to everyone who allows himself to be open. In the ongoing possibility to learn without limitation from experience, having the free will to learn from 'errors' or not, liberation from evil is found.

This is the royal science, the royal secret, the highest purifier, the understanding [is] clear, lawful, very easy to do, imperishable. BG9.2

9.2 There is only one law.

Comment: We can only assimilate and work with differences, creating space-time in the re-choices of limitations to express ourselves, resulting in cause and effect. One law only!

This whole world is diffused by Me in unmanifest aspect. All beings are abiding in Me, but I am not abiding in them. BG9.4

9.3 This whole world is pervaded by THAT in the unmanifest aspect. All beings abide in THAT, but THAT does not abide in them.

Comment: The world, that play of *manifest–dissolution*, is pervaded by THAT as the unmanifested assimilated difference of *manifest–dissolution,* the ongoing circular flow of formless into form, of form into formless. The manifest, being limited, is too restricted for THAT.

And beings are not abiding in Me. See My royal Yoga! Supporting beings and not residing in beings is My Self, creating all beings. BG9.5

9.4 And the beings do not abide in THAT, although THAT supports the beings but does not abide in the beings; THAT is the origin of the beings.

Comment: By bending over itself in the investigation of its manifestation, THAT originates the interplay of *form–formless,* of *spirit–matter.* In that ongoing assimilation of differences, THAT originates the beings and supports them but is not limited by them. Originating implies an ending, so the beings do not remain in THAT, which is beyond space-time. The answer to the question: 'to be or not to be', is found in OG9.3 and OG9.4 as 'to be and not to be'. When free of the pairs-of-opposites *to be–not to be,* one lives the implied third: that what makes free, living and dying in the Now.

As the great wind, going everywhere, always abiding in space, so are all beings abiding in Me. Consider this! BG9.6

9.5 Just as space pervades beings, supports them and is the origin, so is THAT.

Comment: In the origination of space-time, THAT reflects itself and in its ongoing reflections, the bearers of formless matterlessness are the images and shadows of THAT. Although no attributes can be attached to THAT, space is like an image of THAT: it has no centre, supports the beings, but still remains itself.

All beings, Arjuna, go to my Material Nature at the end of a Kalpa; I create them again at the beginning of a Kalpa. BG9.7
Resting on My Material Nature, I create again and again this whole multitude of beings without free will from the power of Material Nature. BG9.8
And these actions do not bind Me, Arjuna; I am sitting indifferently, unattached to these actions. BG9.9

9.6 All beings return to the Primordial Substance and are born from it; the inevitability of the breathing of the universe creates and dissolves, without manifestation of the unmanifest, according to life's will to act.

Comment: The will of Life is found in the inevitable action where action and non-action are equally valued, that ongoing movement of realization of the differences between form and dissolution without revealing the unmanifest. The assimilation of differences, the bringing into equilibrium of differences, creates other differences, always in movement, always in the inevitable breathing of creation and dissolution, that wheel of Life that turns in THAT. All beings, the images and shadows of THAT, are THAT expressing in inevitable action, until the beings re-unite in the Primordial Substance by fully releasing their limitations and are reborn from it by the fire of the Primordial Spirit in the investigation of THAT.

With Me as overseer, material nature produces the moving and unmoving. With this cause, Arjuna, the world revolves. BG9.10

9.7 The Primordial Substance produces the moving and unmoving, with THAT as the cause.

Comment: In investigating its manifestation, THAT reveals itself in Spirit and Substance. Forced by the movement of the fire of the Primordial Spirit, the Primordial Substance reflects moving and non-moving.

Fools despise Me, dwelling in human form, not knowing My higher nature: the great Lord of beings. BG9.11

9.8 Fools misjudge THAT, dazzled by the form.

Comment: Form, created in the flow of re-choices of limitations, dazzles in its manyness. Fools identify themselves with form in all its aspects, not seeing the ongoing movement of manyness into Oneness and back into manyness without revealing THAT. They misjudge THAT in their bondage to the images and shadows of THAT.

They are of vain hopes, vain actions, vain knowledge, absent-minded, devilish and demoniac, and even clinging to a delusive nature. BG9.12

9.9 Their knowledge, their minds, and their actions are vain.

Comment: Vain is knowledge, vain is a mind that has preferences for Substance or Spirit, ignoring the interplay of both expressed in their difference. Knowledge becomes wisdom by applying it. Vain are the actions that ignore the interplay of Spirit and Substance, of Substance and Spirit. Action based on a one-track mind does not flow, does not bring harmony to itself, in society, in nature, or in the universe.

And by the sacrifice of knowledge, also others, sacrificing, honour Me as the Oneness, as the fragmented and the manifold omnipresent. BG9.15

9.10 By performing action with knowledge, others recognize the Oneness, the multiple, and the manifold omnipresent THAT.

Comment: By doing inevitable actions, by pouring the content of our being into the action, in assimilating in Oneness the differences found in the manyness and passing it on into manyness again without attachments, without personal desires, the flow of Life is not disturbed, and others can easily acknowledge the harmony of Spirit and Substance in awareness of the manyness and distinctness, those images and shadows of the omnipresent Oneness THAT.

The knowers of the three Vedas, the soma drinkers, [their] evils purified, worshipping Me with sacrifices, they wish to go to heaven. They, attaining the pure world of the Lord of the gods, enjoy the divine pleasures in heaven. BG9.20

9.11 Those who know the three attain realization of existence by THAT.

Comment: He who knows and understands that in the re-choices of limitations arise time realization in the Now, the three worlds: *past–present–future,* he becomes aware of existence by THAT, seeing time as the inevitable expression of eternity and vice versa.

Having enjoyed the vast world of heaven, when [their] merit is exhausted, they enter the world of mortals. Thus, following the law of the three Vedas, desiring the objects of desire, they obtain going and coming. BG9.21

9.12 When their merit is exhausted, they re-embody themselves.

Comment: All the life experiences are gathered while dying. In being dead, they are examined as if we are listening to the dissonants for improvement, purification and harmonization of our total experiences. A mirror is not clean until the last spot has been wiped away. One re-embodies oneself in order to do so, after having balanced and exhausted all one's merits.

Thinking on no one else, those men worship Me. For them, for the constantly disciplined, I conduct the safekeeping of [their] property. Even those devotees of other gods [who] offer endowed with faith, even they offer to Me alone, Arjuna, [though] not according to the rule. BG9.22/23

For I am the enjoyer, and indeed, the Lord of all sacrifices. Though, yet they do not really recognize Me; hence they fall. BG9.24

9.13 THAT is the same for all; those who deny THAT fall until they recognize THAT. Fortunate is he who directs his will to know THAT. Joy and freedom beckon to him.

Comment: Expressing itself, mirrored in the cyclic flow of emergence and dissolution, THAT is omniscient and therefore equal to all. The spark of THAT is in all and in everything, and so is the bliss of silence, that flame of love, also available and open to each and everyone. We fall if we hold to the spirit or to matter as separate entities. In the assimilated difference, the simultaneity of both opposites, *limited–unlimited, unperishable–perishable, Spirit–Substance,* are expressed as Oneness, and peace and liberation is found.

10 The Power of power development

Neither the hosts of gods nor the great seers know My origin, for I am in every respect the beginning of the gods and the great seers. BG10.2

10.1 The origin is unknowable: 'the THAT'.

Comment: To know is expressing a difference and implies limitation. The origin cannot be limited.

He who knows Me, the unborn and the beginningless, the great Lord of the world, he, unconfused among mortals, is released from all evils. BG10.3

10.2 Know THAT as unborn, without beginning, without end.

Comment: Unlimited, whole, beyond time, yet mirroring time in eternity, THAT IS, not limited by time.

He who knows this manifestation of power and Yoga of Me in truth is endowed with steady Yoga; there is no doubt [about this]. BG10.7

10.3 He who knows the expansion and contraction of THAT is holy.

Comment: The cyclic flow of emergence and dissolution in THAT, without revealing THAT, the flow of manyness into Oneness and into manyness again in full contact with the wholeness as reflections and shadows of THAT, is the ongoing flow of Life leaving the ISness unfragmented.

I am the origin of all; from Me all proceeds. Thinking thus, they honour Me, the fully aware intelligent ones. BG10.8

10.4 THAT is the origin of all and to THAT all returns.

Comment: The origin is unknowable, is whole. THAT wholeness is reflected in all manifestations, so there has never been a separation from THAT.

11 Striving for Oneness by contemplation of form

Behold My forms, Arjuna, by the hundreds or the thousands, various creations, divine and of various shapes and colours! BG11.5

11.1 The forms of THAT are uncountable, visible and invisible, colour and sound.

Comment: This chapter indicates that striving for Oneness can also be achieved by studying the essence of the uncountable forms, by studying physics. Light in its different colours, oscillating electric and magnetic fields, and sound, those collective movements of molecules, are all expressions of reality. Sound and light are found everywhere, be it large or small, in life and relationships. Even black holes have their acoustic counterparts. Waves, ripples in a stream, behave much like light waves in space-time. The flow of the stream around a rock is not uniform, so the ripples are bent and their wavelengths vary. The same happens to light passing through the gravitational field of a planet or star. In some cases, the flow is so fast that ripples cannot propagate upstream—just as light cannot propagate out of a black hole[45].

45 Jacobson, T. A., and R. Parentani, 2005, 12: 49–55.

I am time, the great cause of the destruction of the worlds, engaged to destroy here in the world. Even without you [Arjuna] they shall not live, all the warriors who are arrayed in hostile armies. BG11.32

11.2 The form of THAT is time, which in its course changes the order of the world.

Comment: The everywhere ongoing re-choices of limitations, that emergence of space-time in the investigation of the cosmos of itself, are reflected everywhere, as well as in the life of each human. In its form continuation, time changes the order of the world, back from the exponential inflation within the first trillionth of a second of the life of the universe, up to its age of 13.82 billion years, and ever expanding into dissolution. Unexpected temperature fluctuations after the inflation were found in the measurement of the cosmic microwave background radiation, the light that fills space from the time that the universe became opaque, 380,000 years from its beginning. Measurement of the cosmic microwave background radiation showed that our universe is flat within 0.1 percent margin of error. Of the universe, 4.9 percent is ordinary matter and 26.8 percent is of a different kind of matter that has gravity, called dark matter as it does not emit light. The temperature of cosmic microwave background radiation dropped from its initial 3000 K to 2.7255 K, with an asymmetry in the average temperature between the two hemispheres of the sky, and a largeish cold spot that defines a preferred direction in space. The size of the universe has expanded since then about 1,100 times and is accelerating due to the 71.4 percent of 'dark energy' in it. Time keeps changing the order of the world from the time of the formation of the first stars, about 400 million years from its beginning, and is still changing the global order of the world while forming and dissolving galaxies, stars, and planets in its ongoing expansion[46].

[46] NASA/WMAP, 2006; ESA, 2013.

12 Striving for Oneness by contraction

Fixing the mind on Me, [those] who are always disciplined worship Me. [Those who] have approached Me with supreme faith they are considered as the most disciplined to Me. BG12.2
But [those] who worship the imperishable, undefinable, unmanifest, the omnipresent and unthinkable, the changeless, the immovable, and the eternal, subduing the senses, always even-minded, rejoicing in the welfare of all beings, they also attain Me. BG12.3/4
Greater is the trouble of those who have fixed their minds to the unmanifest, for the goal of the unmanifest is difficult to attain by the embodied. But who, renouncing all actions in Me, having Me as the highest, they worship, meditating on Me with truly undistracted Yoga, for those, whose minds have entered into Me, I am soon the deliverer from the ocean of death and transmigration, Arjuna. BG12.5–7

12.1 They who see THAT as Oneness, the imperishable, undefinable, unmanifest, omnipresent, unchangeable, immovable, a lasting multitude, become unboundedly aware of THAT.

Comment: The many descriptive words used to suggest the unlimitedness of THAT do not even approximate THAT, which cannot be given attributes, which is beyond the cyclic movement of *manyness–Oneness*, beyond the manifest and unmanifest; expressing ISness in allowing the space for the movements of Changeful Changeless, without revealing ISness. Becoming conscious of the interrelation of THAT and Oneness, one becomes *un*bounded aware of THAT.

Fix your mind on Me alone, cause to direct your intelligence to Me! Without a doubt, you shall indeed dwell in Me hereafter. But if you cannot fix the mind steadily on Me, then seek to attain Me by the repeated practise of Yoga, Arjuna! If you are unable even of repeated practise, be devoted to work for Me! Even by performing actions for My sake, you shall attain perfection. But if you are unable even to do this, then resorting to My Yoga, abandoning all the fruits of action, act with the self restrained! For knowledge is better than practice; meditation is superior to knowledge; abandonment of the fruit of action is better than meditation; from abandonment immediately [comes] peace. BG12.8–12

He who dislikes no being, [is] friendly and compassionate, truly free from all worldly connections, humble, indifferent to pain and pleasure, patient, the Yogi, always contented, the self restrained, of firm resolve, the intellect and mind fixed on Me, who is devoted to Me, he is dear to Me. He from whom the world is not afflicted, and who is not afflicted from the world, who is freed from joy, impatience, fear and distress, he is also dear to Me. BG12.13–15

[He who is] indifferent, pure, capable, free from affection, free from anxiety, abandoning all undertakings, who is devoted to Me, he is dear to Me. He who neither rejoices nor hates, nor mourns nor desires, abandoning good and evil, who is full of devotion, he is dear to Me. Alike to foe and friend, and so also in respect and disrespect, alike to cold and heat, joy and sorrow, freed from attachment, equal to blame and praise, silent, content with anything whatever, [is] homeless, steady-minded, full of devotion, that man is dear to Me. BG12.16–19

But they who worship this nectar of duty as declared, faith holding, having Me as the highest; those devotees are more than dear to Me. BG12.20

12.2 Concentrate your thinking on THAT, focus your intelligence on THAT with all your will and control of your thoughts.

Comment: Turn inside to the realms of silence, release tension while restraining wandering thoughts, let go those self-imposed limitations, open yourself to the light that is already in you.

13 Striving for Oneness by the distinction between the observed and the observer

This body, Arjuna, is called the field. Thus, he who knows this is called the knower of the field by the knowers of That. BG13.1
Know also that I am the knower of the field in all fields, Arjuna! Knowledge of the field and of the knower of the field, that is considered by Me as knowledge. This field, what it is and of what kind, what its modifications are and whence, which, and what This [is] and what its power is, that, in brief, hear from Me! It has been sung in many ways by the seers with various sacred hymns one by one, and even with lines of well-founded and ascertained Brahman aphorisms. The great elements, 'I-making', intelligence, and even the unmanifest, and the ten senses, the One, and the five objects of the senses, BG13.2–5

13.1 The great elements, sense of 'I-ness', the intelligence, the unmanifest, the ten (the senses and their organs of action), the One, and the five objects of the senses with their modifications and actions, are the field of observation in reciprocal action with the observer; and one has to know these.

Comment: The verse enumerates the elements to know. We have to know the material world expressed as *earth–water–fire–air*. We need to be aware of our limitation in 'I-ness', of intelligence, and of the unmanifest in the cyclic flow of emergence and dissolution; to perceive the sense organs: eye, ear, skin, tongue, nose, and experience the organs of action: hand, foot, mouth, anus, and genital organ. We have to be aware of the workings and wanderings of the mind, and of the five objects of the senses: sight, hearing, touch, taste, and smell with all their interactions. We have to know these elements to assimilate the difference in *observer–observed* properly.

Desire, hatred, pleasure, pain, bodily mass, intelligence, firmness, this is briefly called the field with its modifications. BG13.6
Humility, sincerity, non-violence, patience, honesty, serving a spiritual teacher, purity, firmness, self-restraint; indifference to the objects of the sense, and free from 'I-making', even consideration of the vice in birth, death, old age, disease, and pain; impassionate, free of attachment to son, wife, home, and so on, and always in equanimity towards desired and undesired events, and with unswerving exclusive devotion to Me, frequenting a solitary place, dissatisfaction in an assembly of men, constancy in the knowledge of the Supreme Spirit, and observing the aim of the knowledge of 'That-ness', this is called knowledge; what is contrary to this is ignorance. BG13.7–11
I shall declare that which has to be known, knowing which, one attains immortality. Beginningless [is] the supreme Brahman. It is called, for that reason, neither existent nor nonexistent. BG13.12
With hands and feet everywhere, with eyes, head and mouth everywhere, with ears everywhere, That stands, covering all in the world. It appears to have the guna power of all the senses, [while] freed from the power of all the senses, even impassionate yet supporting all, without guna yet experiencing guna, outside and inside beings, unmoving as well as moving, and from its subtlety, That is unknowable. That is far away and also near. BG13.13–15
Undivided yet standing as if divided in beings, this is to be known as the supporter of beings, [their] devourer and creator. Indeed, this is the light of lights, said [to be] beyond darkness, knowledge, the to-be-known, and [what] is understood by knowledge, being in the heart of all. Thus the field, knowledge, and the to-be-known, is briefly described. My devotee, understanding this, enters into My state of being. BG13.16–18

13.2 The proper distinction between field and knowledge of the field, the observed and observer in their reciprocal action, gives knowledge of the Self.

Comment: The Oneness of space and the manyness of limitations in space evolving into Oneness again, an equilibrium of manyness in Oneness, as the assimilated difference in the reciprocal distinction of the observed and the observer, lead to the awakening of the unlimited Self.

Indeed, know that material nature and Spirit are both without beginning, and indeed, know also that the modifications and the gunas arise from material nature! BG13.19

13.3 Know that the Primordial Substance and the Primordial Spirit are both without beginning, and that the modifications and Basic Attributes are manifestations of the realizations of both in non-separation, as active distinctions.

Comment: Substance and Spirit are without beginning or end. The eternal image of Spirit is found in the time measure of Substance and vice versa, the unseparated mirroring of Spirit and Substance. Substance as time manifestation, and Spirit as eternity manifestation are distinctions in Oneness, manifested by limitation. The awareness of both unseparated is found in the conscious assimilation of their difference in time and eternity.

The material nature is called the cause of agency, instrument and doer. The Spirit is called the cause in the experience of joys and sorrows. BG13.20

13.4 The Primordial Substance is called the cause of agency, instrument and doer. The Primordial Spirit is called the cause of the experience of joy and sorrow.

Comment: The space-time manifestation in Oneness mirrored in time, called Substance, leads to the birth-states in the ongoing flow of cause and effect. In this process the Primordial Substance is seen as an instrument and a doer causing actions. Spirit, the space-time manifestation in Oneness mirrored in eternity, gives the experience of pleasure and pain as adjudged by 'I-ness'.

For the Spirit, residing in material nature, enjoys the gunas born from material nature. Its attachment to the gunas is the cause of births in good and bad wombs. BG13.21

13.5 Then the Primordial Spirit, residing in the Primordial Substance, enjoys the Basic Attributes born from the Primordial Substance. Attachment to the Basic Attributes is the cause of re-embodiment.

Comment: In the re-choices of limitation, that performance of the Spirit, emanate manifestations in space-time. Substance is the time measure of eternity, the mirror image of Spirit. The three Basic Attributes: Perseverance Power, Equilibrium Power, and Movement Power stand here for past, present, future. Attachment to the time aspect without living the eternity aspect is cause for re-embodiment. (See 14.2 for the Three Basic Attributes.)

Witness, consenter, supporter, enjoyer, great Lord, and also supreme Self: thus is called the highest spirit in this body. He who thus knows the Spirit and material nature along with the gunas, existing in whatever way, also he is not born again. BG13.22/23

13.6 He who knows the Primordial Spirit and Primordial Substance with their Basic Attributes does not re-embody.

Comment: When and if the images and shadows of time and eternity, the reflections of Spirit and Substance, of Life, in Changeful Changeless have been fully lived and understood in their movement of realization of differences in the assimilation of both manyness and Oneness, then there is no need for re-embodiment in this world.

Whenever any being is born, moving or stationary, know that [it is] from the union of the field and the knower of the field, Arjuna! BG13.26

13.7 Whenever a being is born, unmoving or moving, know that it is not the union of the distinct, unseparated observed and observer as realization of the Primordial Spirit and Primordial Substance.

Comment: Being born is a next step on the path of striving for Oneness, the path that leads to union by the assimilation of the difference in the triunity *observed–difference–observer*, as realization of the Spirit and the Substance, to awake cosmic realization. Being born shows that that union is not yet obtained.

He sees, who sees that actions are performed entirely by material nature alone, and thus the Self as non-acting. BG13.29

13.8 The Primordial Substance acts visibly. The Self does not act.

Comment: Manifestations in space-time are visibly observed differences. The visible mirrors itself in the invisible. The Self IS.

When one sees the distinct state of being in the One, and the expansion from that alone, then he attains Brahman. BG13.30
This imperishable highest Self is beginningless, without gunas; even abiding in the body, Arjuna, it does not act nor is it defiled. BG13.31

13.9 When one sees the fragmented existence of beings in the One, because no beginning and no properties are able to be assigned to THAT, one sees the non-acting highest Self.

Comment: Beings behave in a fragmented way, but we can be aware of the Oneness in that behaviour without assigned judgements and qualities, just as when drinking lemon juice we know that it is lemon juice by its taste. We have not assigned qualities to the juice; the qualities of the lemon tree and its fruit have resulted in the taste of lemon juice, without our input. So taste life like that and see that in the realization of differences the results of all qualities are found. Be aware that we have to breathe and live in All, and All in us; let us enjoy the Oneness, and not live in a fragmented way. In the One the many are reflected, as are the many in the One. In the difference, the essence of Life can be tasted by not assigning qualities or beginnings, but simply by living ISness. As above, so below. Do not separate the self from the Self, then you live THAT, with no attributes, no beginnings; ISness in the assimilation of the difference of All and Nothing.

14 Striving for Oneness by the distinction of the Three Basic Attributes

Resorting to this knowledge, entering My nature, they are not born even at the creation of the world, nor are they disturbed at the dissolution. BG14.2

14.1 If one has made oneself familiar with this wisdom in practice, so one is not reborn in the creation, nor disturbed in the dissolution.

Comment: By applying knowledge and understanding in THAT by pouring one's being totally into the ISness of Life, in living and understanding Life, only then there is no need to re-embody, since the mirror is clean and no disturbance will occur again in dissolution.

Sattva, Rajas and Tamas, the gunas arisen from material nature, bind the imperishable embodied one in the body, Arjuna. BG14.5

14.2 Equilibrium Power, Movement Power, and Perseverance Power are the Three Basic Attributes born from the Primordial Substance. They bind the imperishable ego in the body.

Comment: In the re-choices of limitation, Substance is manifested in its time attributes: Perseverance Power–Equilibrium Power–Movement Power or *past–present–future.* In each re-choice we have bound ourselves in space-time; we have created a past and a future in the realization of the present in timefull eternity, the ongoing movement of the creator of realization, time, the eternity of difference-realization.

Of these, Sattva is free from impurity, illuminating, and free from disease. It binds [one] by attachment to pleasure, and by attachment to knowledge, Arjuna. BG14.6

14.3 Equilibrium Power seeks the reciprocal resonant vibration with the universe.

Comment: The Equilibrium Power is in the present. The Now, the focus of the mutual reflections of Spirit and Substance in time, is intangible, just as the present is the equilibrium of the past and the future (see Figure 2.1). In putting a limitation we become aware of the manifestations. This difference-realization is already past; the Now has already gone and cannot be altered or stopped. Therefore, avoid all causes and attachments. We are subject to the law of cause and effect, to the form expression of THAT, the reality of the hammer that hits your thumb, but we can search through our understanding to let go all fixations and enjoy the infinite space-unlimited, whole, as the image and shadow of the universe.

Know that Rajas is characterised by passion arisen from attachment to avidity. It binds the embodied one by attachment to action, Arjuna! BG14.7

14.4 Movement Power is the fire of creation, the desire to act.

Comment: Movement Power is future-driven. The whole past assimilates with the present and in this mutual reflection originates the future. Past and present produce the future, resulting in action-driven movement.

But know [that] Tamas is born of ignorance, confusing all embodied ones. It binds [one] by negligence, sloth, and sleep, Arjuna! BG14.8

14.5 Perseverance Power illuminates in the form the rigidity of the desire to act.

Comment: Perseverance Power holds to the past. Incorporating the future into the present results in the realization of the past. Since the past originates in the mutual reflection of the future and the present, it is never fixed and is only partly old. So nothing remains in the same state and even the past is in eternal movement. Holding to the past is trying to take away the motion of time, and without motion, time is time no longer.

Sattva causes attachment to happiness, Rajas to action, Arjuna, but Tamas, is veiling knowledge, and causes attachment to negligence. 14.9

14.6 Equilibrium Power is happiness in realization. Movement Power couples with action. Perseverance Power veils knowledge.

Comment: Living in the present, assimilating the future and the past in the flow of Life without causing disturbances of this flow by attachments and desires, the Power of Equilibrium brings happiness in realization. The Power of Movement yields future-driven actions by the realization of the past in the present. In Perseverance Power, inertia can come in if the unconscious past, holding onto old knowledge, overwhelms the realization of what is possible, and therefore leads to obfuscation of knowledge and prevents growth.

Overpowering Rajas and Tamas, Sattva arises, Arjuna; indeed likewise, Rajas, [overpowering] Sattva and Tamas, and Tamas, [overpowering] Sattva and Rajas. BG14.10

14.7 These Three Basic Attributes are distinctive attributes of Oneness.

Comment: This verse summarizes the idea that the distinctions in time, *past–present–future*, are entangled and arise from and by each other in the mutual awareness of each difference involved. All are aspects of space-time realization and no action anywhere in the universe can become conscious without the three powers: Perseverance–Equilibrium–Movement.

And thus, when the light of knowledge appears in all the openings in this body, then let it be known: Sattva [is] powerful. BG14.11

14.8 By research and knowledge, the wise one acknowledges that Equilibrium Power is purity.

Comment: Purity is living in the Now, the ongoing flow of Life.

Greed, activity, the undertaking of actions, restlessness, desire; these arise when Rajas is powerful, Arjuna. BG14.12

14.9 The aspects of Movement Power lie in desire.

Comment: Not seeing the ISness and wanting to change the direction of the flow of Life is rooted in desire.

Darkness and inactivity, negligence and even delusion, these arise when Tamas [is] powerful, Arjuna. BG14.13

14.10 The aspects of Perseverance Power lie in obfuscation of knowledge, in delusion.

Comment: The delusion that we can hold onto the past, trying to cause time to stand still, results in the obfuscation of knowledge. It often arises from the tendency to apply old well-known knowledge and avoid learning new knowledge that emerges in the flow of time.

But when the embodied one goes to dissolution when Sattva is in power, then he enters the pure worlds of those who know the highest. Going to death in Rajas, he is born among those attached to action; likewise, dying in Tamas, he is born in the wombs of confused ones. BG14.14/15
They say the fruit of well-done action is sattvic and pure, but the fruit of Rajas is sorrow, [and] the fruit of Tamas is ignorance. From Sattva arises knowledge, from Rajas greed; from Tamas arise negligence and delusion arise, and even ignorance. [Those] established in Sattva go upwards, the rajasic remain in the middle; the tamasic, established in the character of the lowest guna, go downwards. BG14.16–18
When the seer sees [there is] no doer other than the gunas, and knows what is beyond the gunas, he goes to My being. The embodied one going beyond these three gunas, the sources of the body, it is freed from birth, death, and old age with sorrows, and attains immortality. BG.19/20
What are the characteristics [of] one who has passed beyond the three gunas, O Kṛṣṇa? What is his conduct, and how does he go beyond these three gunas? BG14.21
He does not hate or desire the presence or absence of light, activity, and even delusion, Arjuna. He who is sitting indifferently, not disturbed by the gunas, [thinking] 'thus the gunas operate', who remains firm and does not move, abiding in the Self, to whom sorrow and pleasure are equal, to whom a clod, a stone and gold are equal, to whom the

loved and the unloved are equal, [who is] intelligent, to whom blame and praise of himself are equal, [who is] equal in respect and disrespect, equal toward the side of friend or enemy, abandoning all undertakings, he is said going beyond the gunas. BG14.22–25
And he who serves Me with the unswerving Yoga of devotion, going beyond the gunas, is fit for becoming Brahman. For I am the foundation of Brahman, the immortal and the imperishable, of the eternal law, and of the happiness of striving for Oneness. BG14.26/27

14.11 The knowledge of the properties of the three, and of the activities in inevitable alliance, gives the 'to BE' as realization of the All.

Comment: In the re-choices of limitation, space-time emerges. With the knowledge of *past–present–future*, knowing the flow of manyness into Oneness and into manyness again as their inevitable connection gives 'to BE' as the time expression of eternity. In the Changeful Changeless, 'to BE' represents the totality of Life as depicted in the left-hand part of Figure 3.3.

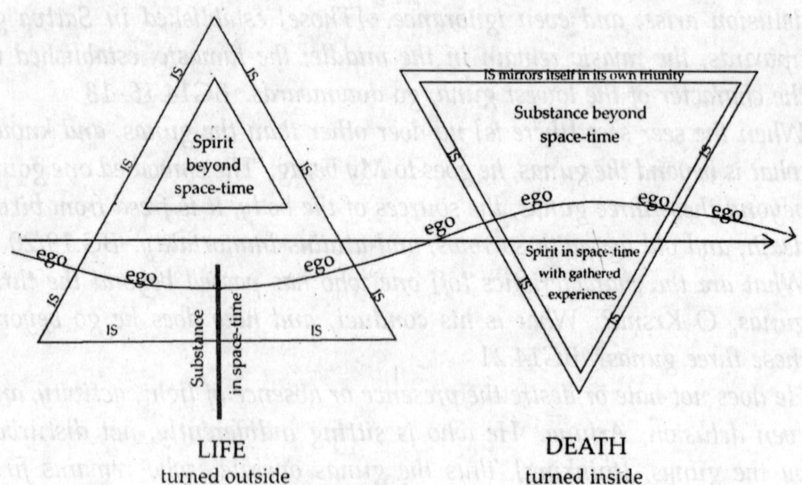

Figure 3.3 Changeful Changeless in IS.

15 Striving for Oneness to the highest Primordial Spirit

They tell of the imperishable asvattha tree, [with its] roots above and [its] branches below, whose leaves are sacred hymns. He who knows this is a knower of the Vedas. BG15.1
Its branches stretched out below and above, grown up by the gunas, [with] the objects of the senses as sprouts; and below, its roots stretched forth, resulting in actions in the human world. BG15.2
So, its form is not perceived here in this world, nor [its] end nor [its] beginning nor [its] foundation. Cutting this asvattha tree, with its well-grown root, by the strong axe of non-attachment; then that path is to be sought, from which, having gone, they do not return again, and so, I resort to that primal Spirit from which ancient activity came forth. BG15.3/4
Without pride or delusions, the sins of attachment conquered, always in the essence of the Self, the desires turned away, freed from the pairs-of-opposites called pleasure and sorrow, the unconfused go to that imperishable path. BG15.5

15.1 Search for the unobservable double image of the 'to BE' in the Self.

Comment: Unobservable Spirit, observable Substance. Observable Spirit, unobservable Substance. Meditate on Figure 3.3 for the double images of reciprocity. As above, so below. In our life, we have to look inside for the 'to BE', and to the Self to become aware of the double image that is beyond time.

Merely a part of Me become an eternal being in the world of living beings. It draws to itself the senses, of which the inner sense is the sixth, abiding in material nature. BG15.7

15.2 Having become an immortal being, it draws to itself the senses (of which the inner sense is the sixth), which are rooted in the Primordial Substance.

Comment: The Self, becoming an immortal being draws the six senses into itself. These six senses: seeing, hearing, thinking and feeling, smelling, tasting acting in the immortal being can become in balance with the two times three 'states', the two double intermingled triangles of life. Time is consciously merged with eternity. Living in the Now, the confirmation of the eternity of man is discovered. In thinking, the mind is rooted in the Primordial Substance. The inevitability of everything takes place in the Self, expressed in the immortal being.

When the individual soul gets a body and also when it steps out, it goes, taking them along from the mind [the feelings and thoughts], like the wind fragrances. BG15.8

15.3 Manas comes and goes like the fragrance of the flowers.

Comment: That thinker, the inner sense that forces us to think, is hard to restrain. We have to bring it under the control of the intelligence of the Self. Its power can easily be felt by trying to think of a dot in emptyness, not allowing any thought to enter the mind. Without practise, soon many thoughts will come and go like the flagrance of flowers. The practises of concentration, meditation and contemplation are needed for restraining the thinker and bring the self under the control of the Self. Then we can be ourselves and are not longer bound by the form manifestations of time or by the Primordial Substance. Moreover, the mind does not show all the collected experiences in life and death.

I, having become the digestive fire, dwelling in the body of the living, with inhaling and exhaling united, I digest the four kinds of food. BG15.14

15.4 After becoming the life-urge or at times the creative-urge, THAT enters the body of the living; with exhalation and inhalation united, THAT digests the four kinds.

Comment: Being in the Now, nothing is left of the pure urge of Life, that manifestation without attachment to form, which can be considered as the inevitability of Life. In the assimilation of the difference in inhalation and exhalation, in the forming and dissolving of the Substance form, THAT manifests itself, while the four kinds [*water–fire–earth–air*, which express all the form possibilities of the world] are digested to release the limitations in thinking of the 'fixed' form and see them in their unlimited reality. Then as the manifestation of Life we become what we are: unlimited, omniscient, omnipresent THAT.

Here in the world are these two Spirits: the perishable and the imperishable, and indeed, all beings are the perishable, the imperishable is called unchangeable. BG15.16

15.5 There are two Primordial Spirits: the changing manifestation and the imperishable, formless, immovable manifestation.

Comment: In the assimilation of their difference, all opposites are unified. To express the unbreakable triunity, both are considered to be 'Primordial Spirits', differentiated as the unobservable and the observable of the manifestation of the Self. Both mirror the Oneness and find their origin in the Self.

But the highest Spirit is another, thus called the highest Self, which, entering, supports the three worlds [as] the imperishable individual Soul. 15.17

15.6 But the highest Primordial Spirit is another, called the highest Self, which is imperishable, which has passed through the three worlds and supports: ⋈

Comment: Higher than the highest Primordial Spirit is another: the highest Self, meaning completely thinking in Oneness, unifying the essence and being of all manifestations. As master of past, present and future, expressing Now, the highest Self transcends the two triunities as the unifying seventh. Here, all flows back into the source of being, to be ejected once again by the essence of All, the movement in Now, as the awareness of difference.

16 Striving for Oneness by the distinction in form and formlessness

Fearlessness, purity of nature, perseverance in Yoga and knowledge, generosity, self-restraint, and sacrifice, and recitation to one's self, austerity, sincerity, harmlessness, truth, free from anger, abandonment, peace, absence of calumny, compassion towards beings, freedom from any desire, gentleness, modesty, steadiness, dignity, patience, fortitude, purity, freedom from treachery, and without excessive pride, [these] belong to one [who] is born to a divine [state], Arjuna. BG16.1–3
Hypocrisy, arrogance, pride, and anger, and even with harshness and ignorance, [these] belong to one [who] is born to a demoniac [state], Arjuna. The divine destiny leads to liberation, the demoniac to bondage. Do not grieve. You are born to a divine [destiny], Arjuna. BG16,4/5
There are two creations of beings in this world, the divine and, indeed, the demoniac. The divine has been described at length; hear from Me about the demoniac, Arjuna! Demoniac people do not know when to be active or inactive, and there is also neither purity nor good conduct nor truth found in them. They say the universe is without truth, having no solid basis, without a Lord; not creating one by the other, it is caused by desire; what else? Holding this view, these lost selves of small intelligence and cruel actions come forth as enemies of the world for [its] destruction. Attached to insatiable desire, filled with the intoxication of hypocrisy, arrogance, and delusion, keeping false conceptions, they follow impure customs. Countless thoughts ending only in death, relying upon the enjoyment of desire [as] the highest aim, thus convinced that 'this is all', bound by a hundred snares of hope, devoted to desire and anger, they long for hoards of wealth by unjust action for the sake of the enjoyment of [their] desire. BG16.6–12
'This is gained by me today, this desire I shall attain, this I have, moreover, even this shall be my wealth. That enemy has been slain by me, and I shall slay others too; I am a master, I am an enjoyer, I am successful, mighty and happy. I am rich, of noble descent; who else is like

me? I shall worship, I shall give, I shall rejoice.' Thus confused by ignorance, bewildered by many imaginings, covered by a net of delusion, attached to the gratifications of desire, they fall into a foul hell.
Self-conceited, puffed up, possessed of pride, arrogance, and wealth, they worship with sacrifices in name only, with hypocrisy, not according to the rule. Clinging to egotism, force, pride, desire and anger, the envious ones hating Me in their own bodies and [in those] of others, in the cycles of rebirth, those haters, cruel, the vilest of men, bad, I forever throw into demoniac wombs. Entering a demoniac womb, deluded birth after birth, truly not coming to Me, Arjuna, thence they go to the lowest path. BG16.13–20
This gate of hell of self-destruction is threefold: desire, anger and greed. Therefore one should abandon these three. A man freed from these three gates to darkness, Arjuna, practises [what is] better for the self, thence he goes to the highest path. BG16.21/22
He who, dismissing the injunction of the scripture, revolves fulfilling his desires, he does not attain perfection, nor happiness, nor the highest path. Therefore, adhering to the scripture as your authority in what is to be done and not to be done, knowing what is said according to the scripture, you should perform action here in this world. BG16.23/24

16.1 The sense of 'I-ness', desire, and impurity by obfuscation of knowledge are the results of holding the form as sole manifestation in high regard. The ignorant ones see the form as the appearance of activity of formlessness. The wise ones see both as realization in the Self.

Comment: High esteem for form manifestation results when we are not aware of the unity in the difference of form and formless, and that differences are created and dissolved in the ongoing motion of assimilating the multitude of differences as expressions of Oneness. Therefore, form is not an activity of formlessness, but in the unity of both, realization in the Self is found in the difference.

17 Striving for Oneness by the distinction of the Threefold

The faith of embodied ones is threefold, born of inherent-self-nature; it is sattvic and rajasic and even tamasic. Now hear this! BG17.2

17.1 The existence of embodied ones is threefold in nature: form – formlessness – and this Oneness.

Comment: Realization needs the inevitability of the reciprocal reflexions of form and formless as differences, but in the assimilation of those differences, the Oneness of form and formless is found.

Everyone's faith is according to Sattva, Arjuna. Man is made of this faith. Whatever faith he [has], so he is. BG17.3

17.2 Truth is personal to everyone's understanding.

Comment: In the re-choices of limitation we create our own world. In that limited world, truth is personal to our own created limitation, to our own measure.

The mindless ones, emaciating within the body the aggregate of elements, and thus Me within the body, know them to be of demoniac resolves! BG17.6

17.3 Self-chastisement of the body is unclean. Mindless ones chastise the house of THAT.

Comment: Thinking that we can become spiritual by denying the body is unwise. Being embodied, the body's maintenance should be in balance with our spiritual life.

But also everyone's beloved food is threefold, likewise their dedication, austerity and generosity. Hear the distinction between them! BG17.7 Foods [that are] augmenting life, energy, strength, health, happiness and satisfaction, [that are] tasty, oily, firm and dainty, are dear to the sattvic. Foods [that are] pungent, sour, salty, very hot, sharp, astringent, and burning, causing pain, sorrow and sickness, are desired by the rajasic. Food that [is] spoiled, tasteless, putrid and stale, unclean leftovers, such food is dear to the tamasic. BG17.8–10

17.4 Eat clean food, think cleanly, live cleanly.

Comment: Clean: being free from personal attachments, free from impurities, which we can become aware of in the slowing down of the flow of our life. Let us choose food that will not imbalance our thinking.

Om, Tat, Sat!, [is] the threefold description of Brahman [as] remembered. By this, the brahmins and the Vedas and the sacrifices [are] ordained up to the present time. BG17.23

17.5 The threefold Brahman is OM, Tat, Sat.

Comment: Life is threefold without manifesting the unmanifest in the difference of the inevitable breath of creation and dissolution of the universe. One is the threefold OM, Tat, Sat. Asat is the mirror of Sat [being], so that Asat is dissolution. Doing Tat is liberation, since then only the differences in Sat and Asat are assimilated without attachments.

Therefore, the acts of sacrifice, generosity and austerity, begin with citing the syllable OM! Discoursing on Brahman is always prescibed by rules. BG17.24

17.6 To understand OM is great. ○ .

Comment: For a discussion of OM, the symbol of Life expressing the ongoing flow of life and death, see page 1–23. The symbol ○ expresses Life as the echo of the universe in its investigation of itself in its created opposite. In this limitation, in the awareness of limited space, infinity is seen, found in the difference created by the limitation. The ○ reflects Spirit and Substance; the unseen centre point defines the circle and vice versa. The centre does not change if the limitation, the circle, is enlarged. The ○ is a perfect sign for Life, for OM.

Tat! Not aiming at the fruit, the acts of sacrifice and austerity, and the acts of various sorts of generosity are done by those who desire liberation. BG17.25

17.7 To do Tat is liberating. ⊙ .

Comment: Tat manifests the difference in Sat and Asat. In assimilating the difference in Sat and Asat, Tat is liberation, since no attachments are involved and the flow of Life goes undisturbed. In ○ the triunity is still unconscious, as the circle reflects infinity inside as well as outside. Although realization of the limitation is shown by ○, we are the unconscious centre, and no restriction is found. With ⊙ the centre is marked and the triunity is only conscious inside the circle; we become bound to our own limitation in the creation of our own world. Since in the re-choices of limitation the dissolution is involved, full freedom is still there, and therefore, Tat manifests in ⊙ Sat and Asat, yet beyond time.

Sat! This is used in the meaning of 'real' and in the meaning of 'good'; likewise, the word Sat is used in a commendable action, Arjuna. BG17.26

17.8 Sat is realization. ⊕ .

Comment: In the limitation ○ the awareness of the difference arises. The difference is perceived as our reality. A limitation has no existence-in-itself and has to be renewed, forced by our inherent self-nature to express wholeness. In this ongoing process, the notion of time arises, which can awaken eternity realization as well. Time, depicted as | on the eternity line —, is the interruption in eternity. Without the eternity line the | represents only the temporal awareness of the manifestation of Life, so both, the horizontal line and the vertical, should be depicted as a cross, because the awakening of eternity is with time realization. Therefore, Sat ⊕ is realization as well as being.

An oblation given and an austerity practised, performed without faith, that is thus called Asat!, Arjuna, and is empty hereafter and empty here in this world. BG17.28

17.9 Asat is dissolution.

Comment: In emptiness, the fullness of life is possible. In Asat there is neither silence or sound, only the ceaseless eternal breathing that does not know itself. There is no time, only unknown duration. Nothing implies All. Both are not known. Sat and Asat are potentialities in the ISness of Life.

18 Striving for Oneness by liberation through renunciation

The enlightened know the renunciation of actions done from desires as renunciation; experts call the abandonment of the fruit of all actions abandonment. BG18.2

18.1 Experts call the abandonment of the fruit of all actions renunciation.

Comment: Being conscious of all differences in the Now, letting the flow of Life be undisturbed, we are not attached to the fruits of all actions. The notion of fruit implies a separation in All IS, and should therefore be abandoned as an attachment.

Hear my decision on abandonment, Arjuna! For abandonment, Arjuna, is declared to be threefold. BG18.4
The act of sacrifice, giving and austerity are not to be abandoned, but rather to be performed; sacrifice, giving and austerity are indeed purifiers of the wise. But also these actions have to be performed abandoning attachment to the fruits. Thus is My conclusion and highest thought, Arjuna. BG18.5/6
But renunciation of an established action is not proper; abandonment of it from delusion is called tamasic. BG18.7
Indeed, it is thus difficult what action one should abandon; he who is merely performing abandonment from fear of bodily pain is rajasic; by no means should he obtain the fruit of abandonment. BG18.8
Thus when that dutyful established action is performed, Arjuna, abandoning attachment and also the fruit, that abandonment is considered as sattvic. BG18.9

The wise abandoner filled with Sattva, [whose] doubt is cut away, does not hate an unfavourable action nor is he attached to a favourable one. For an embodied one is not able to abandon actions entirely, but one who is an abandoner of the fruit of action, he is thus called an abandoner. The fruit of action is threefold in the life to come for those who do not abandon: unwishred, wished and mixed, but never for the renouncers. BG18.10–12

18.2 Renunciation is threefold: of the Equilibrium Power, of the Movement Power, and of the Perseverance Power. Those with bodies are never able to renounce entirely. The required actions in threefoldness have to be done in renunciation.

Comment: Attachments are time-bound. They disturb and bend the flow of Life. Mixing past, present and future in the Now prevents living completely in the Now. Then our realization is bounded by this circle and only if we can let go of our attraction to attachments, the circle of our realization will widen and we can spiral to live in a larger circle of limitation. Being in the body, we are time-bound, and we cannot renounce entirely. But, by completing required actions, we can strive for Oneness.

Learn from Me these five causes, Arjuna, as taught in the Sāṃkhya doctrine for the perfection of all actions! BG18.13
The seat, so the doer, the various organs and the manifold of separate activities, and then only fate [as] the fifth. BG18.14

18.3 The Philosophical System teaches five causes of action: the body, the doer, the organs, the activities, the urge to act.

Comment: In the line of cause and effect, the causes of action for embodied ones, not free from attachments to the fruits of actions, are enumerated in this verse.

Whatever act man undertakes with body, speech or mind, either right or wrong, these five are the causes of it. BG18.15

18.4 Whatever act man performs with body, speech or intellect, these five are the causes of it.

Comment: This verse emphasizes that no more than the five listed causes of action are involved in the actions of man.

This being so, but he who sees himself as the sole doer due to imperfect intelligence; he does not see, the fool. BG18.16

18.5 One with an undeveloped intelligence sees oneself as the doer of it.

Comment: Being in the ISness of Life, we do not disturb the flow of cause and effect; we are active, but we are not the doer of inevitable actions. Our inherent-self-nature urges us on.

Knowledge, the knowable, and the knower are the threefold impulse to action. Instrument, action, and doer are thus the threefold constituents of action. BG18.18

18.6 However, knowledge, the knowable, and the knower are the threefold impulse to action. Instrument, action, and doer are the threefold constituents.

Comment: Knowledge is the assimilated difference in the Spirit triunity *knowable–knowledge–knower*, it is the impulse to action of the assimilated difference in the Substance triunity *instrument–action–doer*. All six listed are interlocked.

Knowledge, action and doer, only in three parts according to the difference of the guna. It is taught in the enumeration of the gunas. Duly hear them also! BG18.19

18.7 These are also called the enumeration of the Basic Attributes in distinction. These parts can be performed in separate actions by biased knowers.

Comment: The six are interlocked: the Spirit triunity and the Substance triunity do not exist as things-in-themselves, but fall into a seventh: the assimilated difference of these triunities in Spirit and Substance. All the triunities are interlocked. Seeing the enumeration as distinctions in Oneness, the basic qualities, *past–present–future,* are then in balance and do not disturb the flow of Life. Those with limited intelligence act separately on these distinctions in the triunities, causing imbalances.

Hear the threefold distinction of the mind and even of firmness, according to the gunas, explained in full one by one, Arjuna! BG18.29

18.8 The mind is likewise threefold: spirit, letter, and stupidity.

Comment: Intelligence can be considered as the unity of the three levels of awareness: superconscious [spirit], conscious [form, perception], and subconscious [body, autonomous system], and it is according to the three Basic Attributes.

That happiness, which is like poison in the beginning and nectar at the end, born from the serenity of one's own mind, is said to be sattvic. BG18.37

18.9 It seems difficult and useless, but the end gives the only happiness of the existence. All the rest is finite in sorrow.

Comment: A living determined by pairs-of-opposites, of separation, of following one side or the other, misses the chance of uniting and becoming what we already are: One. That Oneness is our heritage. Realizing that we are One starts by becoming aware that in assimilating the inevitable difference, there is only Oneness, manifested as manyness.

There is no being, either on earth nor again in heaven among the gods, who would be set free from these three gunas, born from material nature. BG18.40

18.10 Nobody is free from the Basic Attributes; therefore learn to know them.

Comment: Time, that notion of limitation in eternity, expressed in the three attributes, *past–present–future*, gives realization of our awareness of existence. Learn to know these attributes of time, *past–present–future*, which are also expressed and known as the Power attributes: Perseverance–Equilibrium–Motion.

In practising one's own perfection in one's own action, a man devoted to his own work finds perfection. Hear how he finds that! BG18.45

18.11 Work according to your characteristic style, in agreement with the teachings. To fall teaches one to rise. Be yourself and let others be themselves.

Comment: In creating the re-choices of limitations, in these acts of space-time creation, we create our own world. Therefore, we have to work to our own characteristics. Hard times are gifts to our self to learn. Be yourself always, keep asking 'What is that?'; and let others, of whom you are part, be themselves. Be yourself, see the space in front, behind, the fathomless depth below you, the Vastness above you. There is no fixed point anywhere. You are in infinite space, alone as all-One, not knowing your velocity, with no beginning and no ending, unlimited. So free yourself from bondage, see the unlimited freedom of your spirit, be that laughing enjoying being that you are, that we are. Be yourself and let others be themselves in unlimited Oneness manifested as manyness.

Glossary

As in many translations, some words have many meanings, and Sanskrit is an ambiguous and flexible language in which words can even have contradictory meanings. The examples below show that many translations are possible, and it is clear that a good understanding of the meaning of a word as well as its context is necessary for a proper translation. On the other hand, the many meanings can also enrich the understanding of a word, particularly when deeper meanings are given along with the simplest ones. In selecting the meanings of the terms from the Bhagavad Gītā used in this glossary, I have used Monier-Williams, *A Sanskrit-English Dictionary*, 1899; MacDonell, *A Sanskrit-English Dictionary*, 1893; H. H. Wilson, *A Dictionary in Sanskrit and English*, 1832; Carl Cappeler, *Sanskrit-Wörterbuch*, 1887; and sources on the Internet. For further understanding I have added explanations, marked by V:, of Sanskrit terms as discussed by Vimala Thakar in her book, *Insights into the Bhagavad Gita*, 2005. If I have chosen a special meaning, not given in the dictionaries, I have italicized that choice with a reference to the verses where it is used. The less frequently used meanings of a word are put between square brackets.

Abhyāsa repeated or permanent exercise, discipline, custom, use, habit; repetition; repeated reading; study; (in **vedanta**) inculcation of a truth conveyed in sacred writings by means of repeating the same word or the same passage; (in **yoga** philosophy) the effort of the mind to remain in its unmodified condition of purity (**sattva**); (in grammar) 'what is prefixed'; (in poetry) repetition of the last verse of a stanza or of the last word of a chapter; [reduplication; the act of adding anything; military practice]. V:

the process of education; it is alive, not as a mere mechanical physical ritual, not a mechanistic repetition, but probing, discovering, going deeper so as to gain more comprehension; re-doing, but not repeating; it is a stroke of genius that, by re-doing the thing that one has accepted doing, for the sake of learning, for the sake of education, for the sake of purification, one acts attentively, lovingly, with all the sensitivity at one's command. Repetition is passivity, re-doing is active alert attentiveness; re-doing is beneficial for learning, for education, with the senses in voluntary restraint; subduing **tamas**, restraining **rajas**, and utilizing the steadiness of **sattva**.

Ānanda happiness, joy, bliss, enjoyment, sensual pleasure; 'pure happiness'; (often at the beginning and end of proper names); name of various authors; a kind of flute; name of several men; name of a country; a kind of house; [(in dramatic language) the thing wished for, the end of the drama]. V: bliss; the union of the uplifted consciousness with the supra-mental or transcendental consciousness; bliss of love and joy; bliss generated by the harmony built into the cohesive orderliness of life.

Ātman [derived from to breathe, to move, to blow] the soul, life, nature, principle of life and sensation; self, the individual soul, abstract individual; essence, character, pecularity; (in compound) 'the understanding, intellect, mind'; the highest personal principle of life, Brahman; [breath; the person or whole body considered as one and opposed to the separate members of the body; the body; effort, the sun, fire, a son]. V: the root of the term means to eat, to devour, to consume, to assimilate; that which assimilates everything; that which radiates the essence of what it has assimilated; consuming everything that exists in the cosmos and expressing it back again; refers to the body, the mind, the brain, to that which holds the body and the mind together; refers sometimes to the physical body, sometimes to the mind, sometimes to the conditionings; sometimes to that ultimate reality, the ground of existence.

Avidyā ignorance; want of knowledge; ignorance together with nonexistence; spiritual ignorance. V: ignorance about the knowable; ignorance about the nature of the self, leading to wrong identification with the ego; ignorance of the truth.

Bhava be!, coming into existence, birth, birthplace, production, origin; well-being, wealth, prosperity, welfare, excellence; name of a deity; [becoming, turning into, being, state of being, existence, life, worldly existence, continuity of becoming; obtaining, acquisition; a god, deity]. V: feeling of egoness; the attribute that has durability.

Brahman (literally: growth, expansion, evolution, development, swelling of the spirit or soul); the one divine essence and source from which all created things emanate of with which they are identified and to which they return; the Self-existent; the Eternal (not generally an object of worship but rather of meditation and knowledge); one of the four principal priests; the class of men who are the repositories and communicators of sacred knowledge, the brahminical caste as a group (rarely an individual brahmin); final emancipation; one who prays, a devout or religious man, a brahmin who knows the Vedic texts or spellings, one versed in sacred knowledge; the Veda; material Nature; the one impersonal Universal Spirit manifested as a personal Creator and as the first of the triad of personal gods; [pious effusion or utterance, outpouring of the heart in worshipping the gods, prayer; the sacred word; the sacred syllable Om; religious or spiritual knowledge; holy life; final emancipation; the sun]. V: non-individuated transcendental consciousness, an indivisible organic wholeness, the transcendental principle of Life; indestructible *sat*, self-generated awareness *cit*, and spontaneous bliss *ānanda*; *sat–cit–ānanda*, the resplendent characteristics of sovereign intelligence manifest in the human body.

Buddhi the power of forming and retaining conceptions and general notions, intelligence, reason, intellect, mind, discernment, judgement; intellect or faculty of mental perception; an opinion, view, notion, idea, conjecture; thought about or meditated on; intention, purpose, design; insight, comprehension, persuasion, perception; [apprehension, understanding; ready wit, presence of mind; impression, belief, notion; right opinion, correct or reasonable view]. V: the intellect; reason, rationality; perceiving the truth, discriminating the true from the false and carving out voluntary disciplines for regulating and moulding inherited conditionings, tendencies, reactions, past knowledge and experience.

Cit to perceive, fix the mind upon, attend to, be attentive, strive after, conceive, observe, take notice of; to be anxious about, care for; to resolve; to understand, comprehend, know; to become perceptible, appear, be regarded as, be known; to observe, perceive, be intent upon; to form an idea in the mind, be conscious of, understand, comprehend, think, reflect upon; to have a right notion of, know; 'to recover consciousness'; to appear, be conspicuous, shine; to be exceptional; to have in view, be desirous of, aim at; [to care for, be anxious about; to treat medically, cure]. V: the handling of past conditions; self-awareness of indestructability; self-awareness contained in that truth which releases a cohesive principle of orderliness in all its movements.

Dharma established order, that which is established or firm, steadfast decree, law, statute, ordinance; usage, practice, customary observance or prescribed conduct, duty; right, justice (often as a synonym for punishment); virtue, morality, religion [V: religion with a capital R; or spirituality; not the formal structured, organized religions that exist in various parts of the globe], religious merit, good works; [the law or doctrine of Buddhism; nature, character, peculiar condition or essential quality, property, mark; characteristic attribute, property; sacrifice; religious abstraction, devotion; a bow]. V: a code word implying the quality of the act of living, the texture, the fibre, the pouring of the wholeness of your being, doing everything that you have to do with a sense of responsibility; your special unique characteristic; the essence of human life; the principle of cohesiveness that helps the cosmic intelligence to sustain built-in orderliness and harmony in the cosmos, in the community or society, where humans live together; living together or sharing life becomes nearly impossible, unless a principle of cohesiveness or a feeling of togetherness exists among the members psychologically, in their perspectives, approaches, and their attitudes.

Guṇa a quality, peculiarity, attribute or property; (in Sāṃkhya philosophy) an ingredient or constituent of **prakṛti**, the chief quality of all existing beings; good quality, virtue, merit, excellence; [a single thread or strand of cord or twine, string of thread, rope; a garland; a bow-string; the string of a musical instrument, chord; a multiplier; species, kind; the secondary or less immediate object of an action; a secondary element, a subordinate or unessential part of any action; the number 3; an epithet; a property or characteristic of all created things; the merit of composition; the peculiar properties of letters; the first gradation of a vowel, the vowel **a**]. V: attribute; there is a world of difference between attribute and quality. Definition in *Webster's Dictionary*: 'attribute: intrinsic inherent quality naturally belonging to a thing or a person. Attribute indicates a characteristic, often an essential concomitant, with which a person or a thing has been endowed'.

Jñāna knowing, becoming acquainted with, (n.) knowledge, higher knowledge (derived from meditation on the One Universal Spirit); [knowledge about anything, cognizance; conscience]. V: knowing and understanding blended into one; knowledge including psychological understanding along with knowing.

Karman act, action, work, esp. holy work, sacrifice, business, performance; office, special duty, occupation, obligation; any religious act or rite; work, labour, activity; the tenth lunar mansion; [medical attendance; action consisting of motion; product, result, effect; organ of sense; former act leading to inevitable results, destiny, fate (as the certain consequence of acts in a previous life)]. V: that which flows from wholeness, the fullness of being; that which is acted upon, that which is done; figuratively used to denote the inheritance, the physical structure, the psychological conditioning; past actions not only of the parents but of the forefathers; the physical structure and the psychological conditioning, the inheritance that one cannot escape; physically, psychologically, metaphysically, a holistic dedication, a *yajña*, a sharing action that you have to go through, that never creates bondage; learning to live every moment and move through every movement with wholeness, not rooted in thought; action going on from inner fullness and wholeness, becoming a virtual meditation; the movement of Life and living as a dynamic meditation, as a self-fulfilled movement; the capacity to sacrifice the content of your being to create something new; the interaction of energy and the result of the interaction; pouring the being in a responsible way with the energy of attentiveness and alertness; energies contained in the body as the Lord of nature; compassion.

Manas mind (in the widest sense as applied to all the mental powers), intelligence, understanding, perception, sense, conscience, will; the spirit or spirital principle, the breath or living soul which escapes from the body at death; thought, imagination, invention, reflection, opinion, intention, wish, endeavour, sentiment, inclination, affection, desire, mood, temper, spirit; [the internal organ of perception and cognition, the faculty or instrument through which thoughts enter or by which objects of sense affect the soul; in this sense **manas** is always regarded as distinct from **ātman** and **puruṣa**, 'spirit or soul', and belonging only to the body, which, like it, is considered perishable].

Māyā illusion, unreality, deception, fraud, trick, sorcery, withcraft, magic; an unreal or illusory image, phantom, apparition; (in compound) false, unreal, illusory; [art, wisdom, extraordinary or supernatural power, creative power; deceit, being only in appearance; duplicity (with Buddhists one of the 24 minor evil passions); (in philosophy) Illusion (identified in **sāṃkhya** with

prakṛti and in that system, as well as in the **vedānta**, regarded as the source of the visible universe); compassion]. V: a code word: everything that has a beginning and an end, everything whose form, shape, size, colour and qualities are conditioned by the laws of physical nature, governed by the law of causation; not absolutely real, not in the sense of false or in the sense of an illusion; attributing permanence to the transitory, which then becomes unreal; measure, the diversity that you see sensually in the manifest world around you; used in the Vedas or the Upanisads to indicate bewildering puzzling diversity, the innumerableness of expressions; the diversity that is the measure of the inexhaustible potential of the unity of Life; the infinite power, the supreme intelligence figuratively personified in the form of Krishna; Krishna is looked upon as personified Supreme intelligence; not literally but figuratively, poetically; indicates the power, the potential, the existential essence of the Supreme Being; not something false or untrue, it is not unreal; a delusion, a kind of screen that comes between you and the real, between you and the truth; the Mother of the Universe.

Mokṣa emancipation, liberation, release from; final or eternal emancipation, release from worldly existence or transmigration; [(in astronomy) liberation of an eclipsed or occulted planet, the last contact or separation of the eclipsed and eclipsing bodies, end of an eclipse; falling off or down; effusion; setting free, deliverance (of a prisoner); loosing, untying (hair); settling (a question); acquittance of an obligation, discharge of a debt; shedding or causing to flow (tears, blood, etc.); casting, shooting, hurling; strewing, scattering; relinquishment, abandonment]. V: the principle of order and harmony of Life, economic security, fulfilment of legitimate desires and ultimate enlightment; liberation of all identification, dispelling of all ignorance including the ego-consciousness; the ultimate liberation; identified, dedicated to the mental body, which is constituted of the past, of conditionings, but which is dedicated and devoted only to Brahman.

Nirvāṇa blown or put out, extinguished (as a lamp or fire), set (as the sun), dead, deceased (litterally having the fire of life extinguished), calmed, quieted, tamed, disappeared; blowing out, extinction, cessation, setting, vanishing, disappearance; (n.) extinction of the flame of life, dissolution, death or final emancipation from matter and reunion with the Supreme Spirit; (with Buddhists) absolute extinction or annihilation of individual existence or of all desires and passions; perfect calm or repose or happiness, highest bliss or beatitude; V: refers to the dimensional transformation, to the mutation of the psyche; is not related to the physical death of the body.

Om a word of solemn affirmation and respectful assent, sometimes translated by 'yes, verily, so be it'; it is also regarded as a particle of auspicious salutation; sound symbol for the Ultimate Reality; as a sacred exclamation may be uttered (but not so as to be heard by ears profane) at the beginning and end of a reading of the Vedas or previously to any prayer; a mystic monosyllable set forth as the object of profound religious meditation, the highest spiritual efficacy being attributed not only to the whole word but also the three sounds *a, u, m,* of which it consists.

Prakṛti cause, original source; nature, constitution, temper, character, disposition; (in Sāṃkhya philosophy) the original producer of (or rather passive power or creating) the material world; (in politics) a king's ministers, the body of ministers or counsellors, ministry; the subjects of a king, citizens, artisans; [making or placing before or at first, the original or natural form or condition of anything, original or primary substance; extraction; fundamental form, pattern; the constituent elements or powers of the state]. V: matter, the fountain of energy that is functioning; the material out of which the universe is made; the source of creation, the source of all actions; the matter and all energies in it, the manifestations of *Purusha*, or *Brahman*, the Supreme reality, the source of all these energies, the source of all matter; primordial substance.

Prāṇa the breath of life, respiration, spirit, a vital organ, vital air, vital breath, vitality; the vital organs or organs of sensation; air inhaled, wind; vigour, vital energy, power, the spirit.

Puruṣa a man, male, human being, a person, an officer, functionary, attendant, servant; a member or representive of a race or generation; primeval man as the soul and original source of the universe; the personal and animating principle in men and other beings, the soul or spirit; the supreme being or soul of the universe; the spirit as passive and a spectator of the Prakṛti or creative force; name of the divine or active principles from the minute portions of which the universe was formed. V: a code word implying the supreme energy of intelligence.

Rajas impurity, dirt, dust, any small particle of matter; impurity, i.e., the menstrual discharge of a woman; the 'darkening' quality, passion, emotion, affection; (in philosophy) the second of the three *gunas* or qualities; darkness or soul-darkening passion; ['coloured or dim space'; the sphere of vapour or mist, region of clouds, atmosphere, air, firmament; vapour, mist, clouds, gloom, dimness, darkness; the dust or pollen of flowers; cultivated or ploughed land, arable land, fields]. V: energy for movement, motion and activity; a mechanical movement that is constantly moving, provoking, imagining; building up aims, objectives and goals for that mental movement.

Samādhi intense application or fixing the mind on, intentness, attention; intense absorption or a kind of trance; profound or abstract meditation, concentration of the thoughts, intense contemplation of any particular object; [putting together, joining or combining with; union, a whole, aggregate; completion, accomplishment; settlement; justification of a statement, proof; agreement, bringing into harmony; a sanctuary or tomb of a saint]. V: a state of stable neural-chemical stillness and sustained passivity; a supra-mental dimension, a supra-cerebral dimension, beyond thought, beyond time, the dimension of utter unconditional surrender of the ego and its activities, the dimension of utter unconditional uninhibited relaxation, non-action; in negative terms: non-physical, non-rational, non-mental; the total silence of the conditioned mind and the total relaxation of the physical body.

Sāṃkhya one who calculates or discriminates well, an adherent to the Sāṃkhya doctrine; [numeral, relating to numbers; rational, discriminative; discriminative knowledge, enumeration; theory concerned with the true nature of reality]. V: reason, the Path of Reason implying knowledge and understanding blended into one, the reunion with reality through reason, through knowledge; path of knowledge, derived from the invisible, unnameable, immeasurable wholeness of reality.

Saṃnyāsa renunciation of the world; profession of asceticism, relinquishment, abandonment of the world; [laying aside, putting or throwing down, abandonment of, resignation; sudden death, giving up the body; complete exhaustion; deposit, trust]. V: the act of focusing the energies upon the essence of existence, truth, awareness and harmony; instantaneous emancipation or liberation, abandoning all claims to the result of action; the proximity to truth, awareness and bliss, through consciousness.

Sat being, existence, occurring, happening, being present; lasting, enduring; real, actual, as anyone or anything ought to be, true, good, right, beautiful, wise, venerable, honest; (m.) a being, beings, creatures; (n.) that which really is, entity or existence, essence, the true being; that which is good or real or true, good, advantage, reality, truth; (in grammar) the terminations of the present participle; well, right; [abiding in; belonging to; living; a good and wise man, a sage; good or honest or respectable people]. V: indestructible truth; indestructible reality; awareness of the transcendental principle of intelligence.

Sattva being, existence, entity, reality; true essence, nature, disposition of mind, character; vital breath, life, consciousness, strength of character, strength, firmness, energy, resolution, good sense, courage, self-command, spiritual or intellectual being; real being; wisdom, magnanimity; (m./n.) a living or sentient being, creature, animal; [(n.) spiritual essence, spirit, mind; the quality of purity or goodness (regarded in Sāṃkhya as the highest of the three **guṇas** or constituents of **prakṛti** becasuse it renders a person true, honest, wise etc., and a thing pure, clean etc.); material or elementary substance, noun; (m./n.) embryo, fetus, rudiment of life; a ghost, demon, goblin, monster]. V: energy for understanding and clarity; radiance of transparent cleanliness, a radiance of brilliance, of intelligence.

Sva own, one's own, my own, thy own, his own, her own, our own, their own, one's self, the ego, the human soul; a kinsman, relative, relation, friend; a man of one's own people or tribe, of one's own caste; one's own goods, property, wealth, riches.

Svabhāva own condition of state of being, natural state of constitution, innate or inherent disposition, nature, spontaneity, impulse; [native place, birthplace; the essence of the Self, the radiation that causes procreation and development of the creatures, called the inevitable action. Supreme Self originating the state of beings and the creative power called action; *inherent-self-nature*: BG5.14, 5.10, 8.3, 17.2]. V: the intrinsic property of a thing, the sense of identity, the sense of entity-ness, of separate existence; the feeling of being an entity, having an identity, independent of, separate from others; when the unlimited becomes limited, when it becomes individualized, that process itself generates this limitation; the supreme reality in the body gets covered up by this cloud of this feel of 'I-ness'; this feel of 'I-ness' looks upon the rest of life as the object: I as the subject and the rest as the object.

Svabhāvāt from natural disposition, by nature, naturally, by own self, spontaneously; from the *inherent-self-nature*.

Svābhāvika belonging to or arising from one's own nature, natural, native, spontaneous, original, peculiar, inherent; name of a Buddhistic school of thought, perhaps the oldest school of Buddhism, which taught that in the universe there is nothing else than **svabhāvāt**, and that difference and non-difference, dualism and non-dualism, are natural.

Tamas darkness, gloom; mental darkness, ignorance, illusion, error; one of the three qualities or constituents of everything in creation (the cause of heaviness, ignorance, illusion, lust, anger, dullness, pride, and solidity, sin, sorrow); [the darkness of hell, hell or a particular division of hell]. V: the principle of steadiness; inertia or passivity that causes laziness, sluggishness, postponement of action, postponement of decision, clumsiness.

Vairāgya disgust, aversion, distaste for or loathing of; freedom from all worldly desires, indifference to worldly objects and to life, asceticism; inwardness. V: renunciation with a positive dynamic interest in the supreme reality enabling one to remain non-attached and non-involved.

Veda knowledge, true or sacred knowledge or lore, knowledge of ritual; name of certain celebrated works that constitute the basis of the first period of the Hindū religion; name of the number 'four'; feeling, perception. V: the works stand for unconditional physic freedom; they cannot stand the touch of bondage at any level, in any manner whatsoever.

Vidyā knowledge, science, learning, scholarship, a discipline of science, esp. sacred knowledge (threefold) or magic, spell. V: knowledge about the knowable, the knowable about oneself, the body, the brain, the mind, and also knowledge about the cosmos.

Yajña worship, devotion, act of worship or devotion, prayer, praise; offering, oblation, sacrifice; [a worshipper, sacrificer, fire; *holistic-dedication*: BG3.9/15, 7.30, 9.15/24, 16.1, 17.7/24/25, 18.5]; V: a code word implying the pouring of the contents of one's own being into every movement, at every moment; every expression is a pouring of the content of your being. Whether you look at a person, or talk to a person, your glance is pouring your being into sight. Words also are a pouring of the content of your being, so don't keep some aspects of your being for yourself; the process of constant sharing without wanting anything back, with the awareness of our inter-relatedness, which is the unity of Life.

Yoga [from the root *yuj*] employment, use, application, performance; a means, expedient, device, way, manner, method; a supernatural means, charm; incantation, magical art; any junction, union, combination, contact with; relation, connection; fitting together, fitness, propriety, suitability; exertion, endeavour, zeal, diligence, care, attention; application or concentration of the thoughts, abstract contemplation, meditation, (especially) self-concentration, application or concentration of thoughts, abstract contemplation; abstract meditation and mental abstraction practiced as a system (as taught by Patañjali and called the yoga philosophy; in the practice of self-concentration it is closely connected with Buddhism); (in astronomy) conjunction, lucky junction; [the act of yoking, joining, attaching, harnessing; a yoke, team, vehicle, conveyance, fixing (of an arrow on the bow-string); a remedy, cure; stratagem, a trick, fraud, deceit; undertakings, business, work; acquisition, gain, profit, wealth, property; occasion, opportunity; partaking of, mixture; arrangement, putting together; disposition, regular succession, any simple act or rite conducive to yoga or abstract meditation; a follower of the yoga system, the union of the soul with nature; (in arithmatic) addition, sum, total, aggregate; (in grammar) the connection of words together, syntactical connection of words, construction, a combined or concentrated grammatical rule or aphorism, the connection of a word with its root, original or etymological meaning; a violator of confidence, spy, constellation; *striving for Oneness*]. V: From root yukta: to connect, to unite; it has the nuance of re-union of that which was separated by an illusion; that which was separated because of the glamour of appearances and the lack of the capacity to discriminate appearances from reality; when separation ends and reunion takes place; implies the science of conjoining the unmanifest to the manifest, the science of joining the awareness of the nature of reality to every movement of your life. The science of yoga starts with an acquaintance of the body and mind, the brain, acquaintance with its mechanism and way of functioning, the inter-relatedness of all the sense organs, the senses, the energies contained in those senses, and their way of functioning. The science of yoga also teaches how to purify the sense organs, so that the energies contained in them can flow harmoniously and smoothly, without any damage or mutilation. It teaches the way to purify the psychophysical structure, containing the conditionings of the past. It helps us to learn to be conscious of the psychophysical structure and to be aware of that which is beyond, behind, beneath the psychophysical structure. It is a science of non-violence with the body, with the brain, with speech, with the movement of relationship. Education is the path of non-violence, of eliminating impurities, imbalances and distortions, healing damage, letting the essential creative energy manifest itself through our being; it harmonizes the unmanifest and the manifest.

Yukta yoked or joined or fastened or attached or harnessed to; prepared, ready; set to work, made use of, employed, occupied with, engaged in, intent upon; absorbed in abstract meditation, concentrated, attentive, disciplined, active; furnished with, endowed or filled or supplied or provided with, accompanied by, possessed of; attended; relating to,· fit, suitable, appropriate, proper, right, established, proved, just, due, becoming to or suitable for, sensible; junction, connection, union; fitness, suitability, propriety; a team, yoke; an officer, official, a civil servant, a clerk; [instituted, zealous, occupied with, absorbed in thought, integrated; ready to, prepared for; skillful, clever, experienced in, familiar with; united, connected, combined, following in regular succession; to come in contact with, (in astronomy) being in conjunction with; (in compound) increased by, added to; connected with, concerning; subject to, dependent on; fitted, adapted, conforming or adapting one's self to, making use of; auspicious, favourable; prosperous].

Bibliography

Arnold, Sir E., *Bhagavadgita*, Dover Thrift Editions, reprint from the 1899 edition, Dover Publications, Inc., New York, 1993.

Belvalkar, S. K., *The Cultural Heritage of India*, rev. ed., Rama-Krishna Mission Institute of Culture, Calcutta, Vol. 2, 1969.

Besant, Annie, and Bhagavan Das, *The Bhagavad Gītā*, Theosophical Publishing House, Adyar, Madras, India, 1926.

Bhagavadgītā, *The Bhagavadgītā: being reprint of relevant parts of Bhīṣmaparvan* from B.O.R. Institute's ed. of the Mahābhārata for the first time crit. ed. by S. K. Belvalkar, Poona, 1945.

Bhagawad Gita, Boedhi Priester Organistie, Jakarta, 1942, 14 pp.

Bhīsmaparvan, The: Being the sixth book of the Mahābharata, the great epic of India. Bhandardar Oriental Research Institute, ed. by S. K. Belvalkar, Poona, 1947.

Bhandarkar, R. G., *Collected Works of Shri R. G. Bhandarkar*, Bhandarkar Oriental Research Institute, Poona, Vol. 1, 1933; Calcutta, Vol. 2, 1969; Poona, Vol. 4, ed. N. B. Utgikar, 1929.

Brockington, J.L., *The Sanskrit Epics*, Handbook of Oriental Studies, 2nd Part: India, 12th Bd, Brill, Leiden, 1998: pp. 267–271.

Buitenen, J. A. B. van, *The Bhagavad Gītā in the Mahābhārata*, The University of Chicago Press, Chicago, 1981.

Cappeller, Carl, *A Sanskrit-English Dictionary*, Karl J. Trübner, Strassburg, 1891.

Chidbhavananda, Swami, *The Bhagavad Gita*, Sri Ramakrishna Tapovanam, Tirupparaitturai, 1979.

Chinmayananda, Swami, *The Holy Geeta*, Central Chinmaya Mission Trust, Mumbai, 2002.

Dasgupta, Surendranath, *A History of Indian Philosophy*, Cambridge University Press, Cambridge, Vol. 2. 1952.

Davies, John, *The Bhagavad Gītā*, Chaukhamba Sanskrit Pratishsthan, Delhi, 2006.

Desai, Mahadev, *The Gita according to Gandhi*, Navajivan Publishing House, Ahmedabad, India, 1946.

Deutsch, E., *The Bhagavad Gītā*, published by Holt, Rinehart and Winston, New York, 1968.

Edgerton, F., *The Bhagavad Gītā*, Harvard University Press, Cambridge, Massachusetts, 1944.

ESA, 'Planck Reveals an almost Perfect Universe'. Website information of March 21, 2013 at http://www.esa.int/Planck.

Ganguli, K. M., *The Mahabharata of Krishna-Dwaipayana Vyasa*, Munshiram Manoharlal, New Delhi, 4th edition, Vol. V, Bhishma Parva, 1981.

Henricks, Robert G., *Lao-Tzu Te-Tao Ching*, Ballantine Books, New York, 1992; The Modern Library, New York, 1993.

Jacobson, T. A., and R. Parentani, 'An Echo of Black Holes', *Scientific American*, 2005, 12: 49–55.

Johnson, W. J., *The Bhagavaḍ Gita*, Oxford World's Classics, Oxford University Press, Oxford, 1994.

Khair, G. S., *Quest for the Original Gita*, 2nd revised edition, Somaiya Publications Pvt. Ltd., Mumbai, 1997.

Kṛṣṇa Balaram Swami, *Śrīmad Bhagavad Gītā: The Song of God*, Mathura, U.P., India, 1991.

Kuiken, Gerard D. C., *Eastern Thought and the Gita: The Original Gita and the Bhagavad Gita Compared*, OTAM Books, Den Haag, The Netherlands, 2012.

Levenson, Lester, *Keys to the Ultimate Freedom*, Sedona Institute, Phoenix, 1993.

MacDonell, Arthur A., *A Sanskrit-English Dictionary*, Longmans, Green, & Co., London, Oxford Clarendon Press, 1893. Reprinted from the 1924 edition as *A Practical Sanskrit Dictionary*, Manohar, New Delhi, 2005.

Malinar, Angelika, *The Bhagavadgītā: Doctrines and Contexts*, Cambridge University Press, 2007.

Mascaró, J., *The Bhagavad Gita*, The Penguin Classics, Penguin Books Ltd., Harmondsworth, Middlesex, 1962.

Mead, G. R. S., and Roy Choudhuri, *The Upanisads*, Theosophical Publishing Society, London, 1896.

Miller, B. S., *The Bhagavad-Gita: Krishna's Counsel in Time of War*, a Bantam Book, Bantam Dell, a division of Random House, Inc., New York, 1986.

Minor, R., *Modern Indian Interpreters of the Bhagavad Gita*, State University of New York Press, Albany, 1986.

Mitchell, S., *The Bhagavad Gita*: Three Rivers Press, New York, a division of Random House, Inc., 2000.

Monier-Williams, Sir M., *A Sanskrit-English Dictionary*, Oxford University Press, Oxford, 1899.

Narla, V. R., *The Truth about THE GITA: a closer look at Hindu Scripture*, Prometheus Books, New York, 2010.

NASA/WMAP, 'New Three Year Results on the Oldest Light in the Universe'. Website information of March 17, 2006 at: http://wmap.gsfc.nasa.gov/results.

Olivelle, P., *The Early Upanisads, annotated text and translation*, Oxford University Press, New York, 1998.

Nikhilananda, Swami, *The Bhagavad Gita*, Ramakrishna-Vivekananda Center, New York, 1944.

Patton. L. L., *The Bhagavad Gita*, Penguin Classics, Penguin Books Ltd., London, 2008.

Radhakrishnan, S., *The Bhagavad Gita*, HarperCollins Publishers India, New Delhi, 1993.

Sargeant, Winthrop, *The Bhagavad Gītā*, State University of New York Press, Albany, 1984, 2009.

Saswitha, *Principles of Thinking*, Proceedings of the XIth International Congress of Philosophy, Vol. II, Epistemology, pp. 59–64, Bruxelles, 20–26 August 1953. North-Holland Publishing Co., Amsterdam, 1953.

——, *Swabhawat, De korte weg tot wijsheid*, Wetenschappelijke Uitgeverij N.V., Amsterdam, 1971.

Saswitha, *Dood gaan, dood zijn*, Wetenschappelijke Uitgeverij b.v., Amsterdam, 1974; *Dying and Being Dead*, written in Dutch.

Seckel, Al, *The Fantastic World of Optical Illusions*, Carlton Books, U.K., 3rd printing, 2004.

Sinha, P., *The Gita As It Was: Rediscovering the Original Bhagavadgita*, Open Court, La Salle, Illinois, 1987.

Swarupananda, Swami, *Srimad-Bhagavad-Gita*, Advaita Ashrama, 3rd edition, Mayavati, Almora, Himalayas, 1922.

Telang, K. T., *The Bhagavadgîtâ*, Sacred Books of the East, Editor: F. Max Müller; J. Legge, reprint of the Oxford University Press, 1882: Motilal Banarsidass, Delhi, 1965.

Thakar, Vimala, *Insights into the Bhagavad Gita*, Motilal Banarsidass Publishers Pvt. Ltd., New Delhi, 2005.

Thompson, G., *The Bhagavad Gita*, North Point Press, a division of Farrer, Straus and Giroux, New York, 2008.

White, David G., *Sinister Yogis*, The University of Chicago Press, Chicago, 2009.

Wilson, Fred D., *Mind Is Time*, Taro, Petersfield, 1986.

Wilson, H. H., *A Dictionary in Sanscrit and English*, 2nd ed., Education Press, Calcutta, 1832.

Zaehner, R. C., *The Bhagavad-Gītā with a commentary based on the original sources*, Oxford University Press, Oxford, 1969.

Index

a
absolute *6, 81*
acquisition *45*
action *3, 11, 12, 14, 15, 16, 23, 44, 57, 60, 71, 74, 98, 105, 115, 122*
five causes of *138*
fruits of *46, 73, 137*
improper *71*
inevitable *54, 55, 61, 62, 64, 72, 73, 76, 77, 79, 83, 84, 86, 87, 88, 99, 100, 101, 105, 107, 139*
non *46, 55, 71, 105*
renunciation of *76*
threefold *138, 139*
alcohol *87*
All *58, 120*
IS *39*
Nothing *22, 24, 26*
Arjuna *xi, 34, 38, 40, 43, 44, 45, 47, 48, 53, 56, 57, 58, 59, 64, 65, 66, 73, 75, 76, 77, 81, 83, 86, 89, 90, 97, 98, 105, 106, 108, 111, 113, 114, 115, 119, 120, 121, 125, 131, 132, 133, 136, 137, 140*
as above, so below *93, 120, 127*
Asat *136*
as below, so above *22, 28*
assimilation *4, 8, 11, 14, 16, 17, 23, 28, 37, 40, 41, 47, 53, 55, 66, 67, 74, 92, 94, 97, 103, 104, 105, 117, 119, 120, 129, 133*
attachment *49, 50, 57, 59, 60, 61, 64, 73, 75, 78, 79, 84, 89, 97, 101, 107, 118, 122, 123, 127, 129, 134, 135, 137, 138*
Attributes *42, 105, 113, 116, 126, 147*
Basic *54, 59, 60, 69, 93, 94, 117, 118, 120, 124, 140, 141*
Three *45, 121*
authority *62*
aversion *62, 97*
awake *52, 119*

b
balance *1, 22, 26, 37, 41, 47, 50, 55, 57, 61, 78, 86, 87, 89, 108, 133, 140*
improper *68*
BE *126, 127*
beings *3, 4, 9, 14, 23, 38, 43, 57, 61, 67, 88, 93, 104, 131, 138*
origin of *104*
Belvalkar, S. K. *31, 33*
be yourself *142*
Bhagavad Gītā *x, 5, 33, 35, 44, 143*
Bhandarkar, R. G. *31, 32*
birth *42, 67, 119*
state *69, 117*
body *14, 16, 26, 37, 40, 54, 73, 78, 79, 86, 90, 98, 99, 121, 125, 129, 133, 138, 139, 140*
maintenance of *55, 87*
Brahman *21, 55, 77, 81, 82, 98, 99, 101, 102, 115, 116, 120, 126, 134, 135, 145*
Brockington, J. L. *31*
Buddhi *5, 48*

c
Cappeller, Carl *143*
caste *34, 58*
cause and effect *13, 14, 16, 44, 55, 61, 70*
Causeless Cause *18, 21*
Changeful Changeless *18, 24, 67, 80, 88, 113*
childhood *37*
Choudhuri, Roy *20*
code language *66, 91*
colour *111*
communication *8*

consciousness *7, 12, 27*
cosmos *79, 97, 98, 99, 144*
  background radiation *112*

d
darkness *4, 84, 100, 102*
Dasgupta, Surendranath *32*
dead *26, 36*
death *21, 42, 67*
delusion *48, 97*
desires *9, 13, 57, 62, 76, 124*
dictionary *143*
  Cappeller *143*
  MacDonell *143*
  Monier-Williams *143*
  Webster's *147*
  Wilson *143*
difference *4, 38, 46, 55, 85*
dissolution *92, 121*
distinction *ix, 3, 8, 55, 69, 92, 117, 124, 134, 140*
doer *79, 117, 139*
do nothing *15, 78*

e
ego *10, 13, 15, 16, 36, 37, 41, 62, 121*
egocentric *8, 60, 68*
eightfold *91*
embodiment *43, 68, 89, 101, 118*
empathy *61, 70*
emptiness *10, 15*
essence
  of action *97, 98*
  of beings *97, 98*
  of elements *97, 98*
  of Self *98*
eternity *13, 43, 117*
evil *47, 63, 73, 80*
existence *12, 16, 38, 107, 120, 133, 141*

f
fear *13, 15, 24, 26, 36, 43, 46, 53, 67, 68, 87, 114, 131, 137*
fire *64, 72, 74, 83, 91, 105, 122*
food *54, 86, 87, 129, 134*
  alcohol *87*
  meat *87*
fools *106*
form *10, 15, 16, 17, 18, 19, 22, 36, 37, 41, 101, 104, 105, 112, 122, 128, 131, 132*
formless *10, 15, 17, 18, 19, 22, 42, 101, 104, 105, 129, 131, 132, 133*
four kinds *129*
freedom *9, 22, 42, 61, 108, 135, 142*

g
Ganguli, Kisari Mohan *33*
goal *23, 78, 80, 90, 101, 102*
God *18, 21, 94*
gravitation *111*
guna *54, 59, 60, 63, 93, 94, 116, 117, 118, 120, 121, 125, 126, 127, 140, 141*

h
hairsplitting *61*
happiness *9, 16, 23, 42, 51, 123*
Henricks, Robert G. *6*
Here and Now *9, 13, 16, 22, 23, 24, 26, 48*
hologram *27*
hypocrite *54*

i
I-making *52, 114, 116*
I-ness *59, 60, 64, 79, 91, 115, 132*
ignorance *45, 58, 60, 81, 94, 102*
illusion *16, 23, 94*
immortal *126, 128*
induction *4*
infinite *10, 23, 122, 142*
inherent-self-nature *80, 99, 139*
insight *61, 62, 84, 143*
intelligence *21, 47, 50, 51, 64, 65, 74, 79, 91, 113, 114, 115, 139, 140*
IS *9, 11, 17, 58*
ISness *42, 72, 109*

j

Jacobson, T. A. *111*
Ježić, M. *32*
Johnson, W. J. *31*

k

karman *147*
Kṛṣṇa *xi, 34, 36, 48, 62, 94, 98, 125, 149*
Khair, G. S. *31, 34*
knowledge *5, 46, 49, 53, 64, 66, 72, 81, 91, 107, 115, 116, 123, 140*
  applied *50, 94*
  boat of *73*
  obfuscation of *125, 132*

l

Levenson, Lester *9*
liberation *70, 76, 137*
Life *3, 20, 22, 23, 26, 28, 36, 38, 40, 46, 52, 57, 62, 88, 101, 105, 120, 126, 135, 137*
light *3, 5, 84, 95, 100, 102, 111, 114, 116*
  oldest of universe *112*
limitation *x, 3, 4, 7, 8, 10, 11, 12, 13, 17, 18, 21, 23, 26, 36, 58, 67, 81, 96, 101, 112, 118, 135, 142*

m

MacDonell *143*
Mahābhārata *x, xi, 31, 32, 33, 34, 35*
Malinar, Angelika *31*
Manas *64, 128, 148*
manifest *4, 7, 11, 13, 16, 20, 23, 26, 39, 40, 48, 66, 73, 93, 121, 135, 142*
Manu *66*
manyness *13, 72, 84, 86, 97, 106, 113, 117, 126, 141, 142*
Mawangdui *6*
Māyā *16, 46, 67, 96, 148*
Mead, G. R. S. *20*
meditation *xi, 27, 51, 89, 98, 113, 114, 127*
merit *108*
middle *17, 20, 68*
mind *25, 89*
mindless *61, 133*
Minor, Robert N. *32, 33, 34*
Monier-Williams, M. *143*

n

Narla, V. R. *31*
night *52*
nine-gated city *79*
Nirvāṇa *6, 32, 81, 149*
non
  being *38*
  doing *15, 34*
  existent *4, 8, 18, 26, 38*
  interference *13*
Nothing *58, 120, 136*
  IS *22, 26, 28*
    All *22, 86*

o

observer and observed *3, 4, 7, 10, 13, 72, 73, 74, 76, 78, 115, 116, 119*
old age *37*
Olivelle, Patrick *20, 33*
OM *25, 134, 135*
omnipresent *9, 10, 18, 20, 23, 26, 55, 74, 105, 113, 129*
One *8, 10, 23, 66, 68, 74, 115, 120*
Oneness *9, 16, 41, 74*
origin *92, 109*
  of the beings *104*
Original Gītā *x, 5, 33*
own measure *10, 11, 133*

p

pairs-of-opposites *5, 6, 45, 66, 73, 76, 97, 104*
Parentani, R. *111*
past, present and future *9, 13, 16, 21, 24, 25, 27, 48, 58, 96, 107, 118, 121, 124, 126, 130, 138, 140, 141*
Patton, Laurie L. *31*

peace *16, 51, 70, 79*
perfection *53, 91, 114, 132, 142*
physics *ix, 111*
pleasure and pain *38, 55, 56, 81, 118*
power *63*
  Equilibrium *93, 121, 138*
  Movement *93, 121, 138*
  Perseverance *93, 121, 138*
practice *61, 77, 89, 90, 114*
prakṛti *147, 150*
purpose *3, 23, 47, 57, 68, 101*

r
rajas *63, 93, 121, 122, 123, 124, 125, 133, 134, 137, 151*
re-embody *41, 43, 61, 68, 90, 101, 108, 118*
realization *72, 75, 96*
relationships *44, 55, 99, 111*
release *9, 10, 13, 17, 36, 50, 61, 70, 114, 129*
religious texts *xi, 14*
renunciation *6, 53, 76, 83, 90, 114, 137*
research *11, 124*
rigidity *123*
ritual *94*

s
Sāṃkhya *44, 49, 53, 77, 138, 152*
Saswitha *x, 5, 27*
Sat *136*
sattva *93, 121, 122, 123, 124, 125, 133, 138, 152*
science *xi, 11, 14, 46, 64, 91, 103*
Seckel, Al *7*
secret *66, 103*
seen and unseen *21, 22, 23, 24, 26*
Self *20, 59, 75, 81, 84, 88*
  highest *120, 129, 130*
  non-acting *120*
  of the world *80*
  purification *75, 79*
self-awareness *98, 99*
self-chastisement *133*
self-restraint *50, 82, 83, 100, 114, 116, 131*
senses *xi, 3, 50, 51, 54, 62, 64, 65, 78, 79, 85, 113, 115*
  five objects *115*
sense, sixth *128*
silence *26, 43, 51, 79, 81, 82, 108, 136*
Sinha, Phulgenda *34*
sorrow *10, 13, 15, 50, 81, 86, 87, 134, 141*
  path of *89*
sound *111, 136*
space *10, 18, 86, 88, 105, 117, 135, 142*
  time *ix, 1, 12, 17, 26, 28, 36, 42, 46, 58, 66, 69, 101, 111, 112, 117, 119, 121, 124, 126*
    beyond *17, 20, 24, 26, 42*
    discrete *26*
    inverted *24*
    unlimited *8*
Spirit and Substance *20, 21, 23, 38, 40, 41, 44, 63, 68, 99, 106, 107, 108, 117, 119, 122, 127, 135, 140*
  Primordial *54, 59, 60, 67, 99, 100, 105, 106, 117, 118, 119, 121, 128, 129*
success *15, 47, 69, 73*
svabhāva *153*
svabhāvāt *153*
swabhava *80, 99*

t
tamas *93, 121, 123, 124, 125, 133, 134, 137, 154*
Tao Tê Ching *5, 10, 15*
Tat *135*
Thakar, Vimala *vii, 35, 143*
THAT *17, 18, 20, 21, 39, 42, 55, 58, 61, 65, 68, 69, 70, 71, 72, 74, 75, 79, 80, 81, 82, 88, 90, 91, 93, 94, 95, 96, 97, 98, 99, 102, 104, 105, 106, 107, 108, 109, 110, 111, 112, 113, 114,*

120, 121, 122, 129, 133
the *65, 67, 109*
THE *41, 42, 81, 94, 98, 100*
thing-in-itself *6, 39, 81*
thinker *51, 59, 65, 128*
thought *10, 16, 21, 24, 25, 27, 28, 54, 60, 61, 73, 79, 82, 86, 88, 114*
steadiness in *49*
threefold *132, 133, 134, 138, 139, 140*
threeness *5, 48*
time, *see also* space-time *12*
to be or not to be *104*
triunity *ix, 4, 5, 6, 7, 9, 13, 18, 20, 22, 23, 26, 39, 45, 48, 59, 66, 76, 78, 119, 129, 135, 139, 140*
truth *20, 21, 34, 38, 48, 66, 68, 78, 102, 131, 133*
personal *133*
twofold *53, 61, 81*

u
universe *3, 14, 78, 103, 105, 107, 122, 124, 134, 135*
flat *112*
unmanifest *46, 59, 65, 66, 74, 93, 96, 97, 99, 101, 102, 104, 105, 115, 134*
Upaniṣad *20, 25, 33*
Īśa *21*
Kaṭha *20, 21, 22, 25, 26*
Māṇḍūkya *25*

v
Vastness *x, 88, 94, 142*
Vedas *45, 46, 100, 127, 134*
virtue *80*

w
White, David G. *31, 34*
Wilson, Fred D. *9*
Wilson, H. H. *143*
wisdom *ix, x, xi, 21, 36, 44, 49, 50, 53, 61, 64, 74, 91, 94, 103, 107, 121*
wise *36, 45, 52, 58, 60, 61, 64, 72, 73, 77, 81, 94, 97, 100, 110, 124, 132, 137*
women *35*
world *15, 36, 53, 55, 59, 93, 112*
human *69*
nature *92*
own *7, 8, 11, 16, 23, 28, 46*
Self of the *80*
three *14, 58, 129*
unseen *21*

y
Yoga *26, 44, 47, 53, 66, 75, 77, 78, 83, 84, 96, 131*
youth *37*

z
Zaehner, R. C. *33*
Zen *22*